Praise for the  es by

BOUND TO DARKNESS

"While most series would have ended or run out of steam, the Midnight Breed series seems to have picked up steam. Lara Adrian has managed to keep the series fresh by adding new characters . . . without having to say goodbye to the original ones that made the series so popular to begin with. Bound to Darkness has all the passion, danger and unique appeal of the original ten books but also stands on its own as a turning point in the entire series with new pieces to a larger puzzle, new friends and old enemies."

—*Adria's Romance Reviews*

"Lara Adrian always manages to write great love stories, not only emotional but action packed. I love every aspect of (Bound to Darkness). I also enjoyed how we get a glimpse into the life of the other characters we have come to love. There is always something sexy and erotic in all of Adrian's books, making her one of my top 5 paranormal authors."

—*Reading Diva*

CRAVE THE NIGHT

"Nothing beats good writing and that is what ultimately makes Lara Adrian stand out amongst her peers.... Crave the Night is stunning in its flawless execution. Lara Adrian has the rare ability to lure readers right into her books, taking them on a ride they will never forget."

—*Under the Covers*

"...Steamy and intense. This installment is sure to delight established fans and will also be accessible to new readers."

—*Publishers Weekly*

Look for these titles in the *New York Times* and #1 international bestselling

Midnight Breed series

. . . and more to come!

MIDNIGHT UNBOUND

A Midnight Breed Novella

(

NEW YORK TIMES BESTSELLING AUTHOR

LARA ADRIAN

ISBN: 1939193184
ISBN-13: 978-1939193186

MIDNIGHT UNBOUND
© 2017 by Lara Adrian, LLC
Cover design © 2017 by CrocoDesigns

www.LaraAdrian.com

Available in ebook and trade paperback. Unabridged audiobook edition forthcoming.

MIDNIGHT UNBOUND

CHAPTER 1

Scythe had been in the dance club for nearly an hour and he still hadn't decided which of the herd of intoxicated, gyrating humans would be the one to slake his thirst tonight. Music blared all around him, the beat throbbing and pulsing, compounding the headache that had been building in his temples for days.

His stomach ached, too, sharp with the reminder that it had been almost a week since he'd fed. Too long for most of his kind. For him—a Breed male whose Gen One blood put him at the very top of the food chain— a week without nourishment was not only dangerous for his own wellbeing, but for that of everyone near him as well.

From within the cloak of shadows that clung around the end of the bar, he watched the throng of young men and women illuminated by colored strobe lights that flashed and spun over the dance floor as the DJ rolled seamlessly from the track of one sugary pop hit to another.

This tourist dive in Bari, a seaside resort town located at the top of Italy's boot heel, wasn't his usual hunting ground. He preferred the larger cities where blood Hosts could be hired for their services and dismissed immediately afterward, but his need to feed was too urgent for a long trek to Naples. And besides, that journey would take him past the vineyard region of Potenza—an area he made a habit of avoiding for the past few weeks for reasons he refused to consider, even now.

Hell, especially now, when blood thirst wrenched his gut and his fangs pulsed with the urge to sink into warm, tender flesh.

A snarl slid off his tongue as he let his gaze drift over the crowd again. Against his will, he locked on to a petite brunette swaying to the music on the far side of the packed club. She had her back to him, silky dark brown hair cascading over her shoulders, her small body poured into skinny jeans and cropped top that bared a wedge of pale skin at her midsection. She laughed at something her companions said, and the shrill giggle scraped over Scythe's heightened sense of hearing.

He glanced away, instantly disinterested, but the sight of her had called to mind another waifish female—one he'd been trying his damnedest to forget.

He knew he'd never find Chiara Genova in a place like this, yet there was a twisted part of him that ran with the idea, teasing him with a fantasy he had no right to entertain. Sweet, lovely Chiara, naked in his arms. Her mouth fevered on his, hungered. Her slender throat bared for his bite—

"Fuck."

The growl erupted out of him, harsh with fury. It drew the attention of a tall blonde who had parked her skinny ass on the barstool next to him fifteen minutes ago and had been trying, unsuccessfully, to make him notice her.

Now she leaned toward him, reeking of too much wine and perfume as she licked her lips and offered him a friendly grin. "You don't look like you're having much fun tonight."

He grunted and glanced her way, taking stock of her in an instant.

Human. Probably closer to forty than the short leather skirt and lacy bustier she wore seemed to suggest. And definitely not a local. Her accent was pure American. Midwest, if he had to guess.

"Wanna hear a confession?" She didn't wait for him to answer, not that he planned to. "I'm not having much fun tonight, either." She heaved a sigh and traced one red-lacquered fingernail around the rim of her empty glass. "You thirsty, big guy? Why don't you let me buy you a drink—"

"I don't drink."

Her smile widened and she shrugged, undeterred. "Okay, then let's dance."

She slid off her stool and grabbed for his hand.

When she didn't find it—when her fingers brushed against the blunt stump where his right hand used to be, a long time ago—she recoiled.

"Oh, my God. I, um... Shit." Then her intoxicated gaze softened with pity. "You poor thing! What happened to you? Are you a combat vet or something?"

"Or something." Irritation made his deep voice crackle with menace, but she was too drunk to notice.

She stepped in close and his predator's senses lit up, his nostrils tingling at the trace coppery scent of human red cells rushing beneath her skin. The rawness in his stomach spread to his veins, which now began to throb with the rising intensity of his blood thirst. His body felt heavy and slow. The stump at the end of his wrist ached with phantom pain. His normally razor-sharp vision was blurred and unfocused.

Usually, in some dark, bizarre way, he relished the sensation of physical discomfort. It reminded him that as dead inside as he might feel—as disconnected as he had been ruthlessly trained to be as a Hunter in the hell of Dragos's laboratory—there were some things that could still penetrate the numbness. Make him feel like he was among the living.

This particular kind of pain, though, bordered on unbearable, and it was all he could do not to grab the woman and take her vein right there in the middle of the club.

"Come on. Let's get out of here."

"Sure!" She practically leaped at him. "I thought you'd never ask."

He steered her away from the bar and out the club's exit without another word. Although the Breed had been outed to their human neighbors for more than twenty years, there were few among Scythe's kind—even a stone-cold killer like him—who made a habit of feeding in public places.

His companion wobbled a bit as they stepped out into the crisp night air. "Where do you wanna go? I'm staying at a hotel just up the street. It's a shithole, but we can go there if you want to hang out for a while."

"No. My vehicle will do."

Desire lit her features as she stared up at him. "Impatient, are you?" She giggled, smacking her palm against his chest. "Don't worry, I like it."

She trailed after him across the small parking lot to his gleaming black SUV. In some dim corner of his conscience, he felt sorry for a woman who valued herself so little that she would traipse off with a stranger who offered her nothing in return for the use of her body.

Or, in this case, her blood.

Scythe had been born nothing better than a slave. Had nearly died one. The concept of taking from someone simply because he had the physical prowess to do it pricked him with self-loathing. The least he could do was make sure that when he took he left something behind as well. The woman would be weak with an unexplainable satisfaction once he was finished with her. Since he was feeling an uncustomary twinge of pity for her, she'd also walk away with a purse fat enough to rent a room for a month in the best hotel in Bari.

"This way," he muttered, his voice nothing more than a rasp.

She took his proffered arm and grinned, but it wasn't the coy smile that had his blood heating. It was the pulse fluttering wildly in her neck beneath that creamy flesh that had his fangs elongating. They punched through his gums and he went lightheaded with the need to feed, denied for too long.

They got into his vehicle and he wasted no time. Pivoting in the seat, he reached for her with his left hand, his fingers curling around her forearm. She uttered a small, confused noise as he drew her toward him and brought her wrist to his mouth.

Her confusion faded away the second he sank his

fangs into her delicate flesh.

"Oh, my God," she gasped, her cheeks flushing as her whole body listed forward.

She speared the fingers of her free hand into his long black hair, and he had to resist the urge to jerk away as blood filled his mouth. He didn't like to be touched. All he wanted to do was fill the gaping hole in his gut until the next time he was forced to feed.

She moaned, her breath coming in quick pants as he drank. He took his fill, drawing on her wrist until he could feel the energy coursing through his body, replenishing his strength, fortifying his cells.

When he was done, he closed the tiny bite marks on her skin with a dispassionate swipe of his tongue as she twitched against him breathlessly.

"Good Lord, what is this magic and where do I sign up for more?" she murmured, her chest still heaving.

He leaned back against the cushioned leather, feeling the calm begin to move over him as his body absorbed the temporary nourishment. When the woman started to shift toward him with drugged need in her eyes, Scythe reached out and placed his palm against her forehead.

The trance took hold of her immediately. He erased her memory of his bite and the desire it stirred in her. When she slumped back against her seat, he dug into the pocket of his black jeans for his money and peeled off several large bills. He tossed them in her lap, then opened the passenger door with a silent, mental command.

"Go," he instructed her through her trance. "Take the money and go back to your hotel. Stay away from this club. Find something better to do with your time."

She obeyed at once. Stuffing the bills into her purse,

she climbed out of the SUV and headed across the parking lot.

Scythe tipped his head back against the seat and released a heavy sigh as his fangs began to recede. Already, the human's blood was smoothing the edge from his whole-body pain. The malaise that had been worsening for the past twenty-four hours was finally gone and this feeding would hold him for another week if he was lucky.

He started up his vehicle, eager to be back on the road to his lair in Matera. He hadn't even pulled out of the lot when his cell phone chirped from inside his coat pocket. He yanked it out with a frown and scowled down at the screen. Only three people had his number and he wanted to hear from exactly none of them right now.

The restricted call message glowed up at him and he grimaced.

Shit. No need to guess who it might be.

And as much as he might want to shut out the rest of the world, Scythe would never refuse the call of one of his former Hunter brethren.

On a curse, he jabbed the answer button. "Yeah."

"We need to talk." Trygg's voice was always a shade away from a growl, but right now the Breed warrior's tone held a note of urgency too. Scythe had heard that same note in his half-brother's voice the last time he called from the Order's command center in Rome, and he could only imagine what it meant now.

"So, talk," he prompted, certain he didn't want the answer. "What's going on?"

"The Order's got a problem that could use your specialized skills, brother."

"Fuck." Scythe's breath rushed out of him on a

groan. "Where have I heard that before?"

Six weeks ago, he'd allowed Trygg to drag him into the Order's troubles and Scythe was still trying to put the whole thing behind him. As a former assassin, he didn't exactly play well with others. He damned sure wasn't interested in getting tangled up in Order business again.

But there were only a handful of people in the world who knew exactly what Scythe had endured in the hell of Dragos's Hunter program, and Trygg was one of them. They had suffered it together for years as boys, and had dealt with the aftermath as men.

Even if they and the dozens of other escaped Hunters didn't share half their DNA, their experience in the labs couldn't make for truer brothers than that. If Trygg needed something, Scythe would be there. Hell, he'd give up his other hand for any one of his Hunter brethren if they asked it of him.

Scythe's preternatural ability to sniff out trouble told him that Trygg was about to ask for something far more painful than that.

"Tell me what you need," he muttered, steeling himself for the request.

"You remember Chiara Genova?"

Scythe had to bite back a harsh laugh.

Did he remember her? Fuck, yeah, he remembered. The beautiful, widowed Breedmate with the soulful, sad eyes and broken angel's face had been the star of too many of his overheated dreams since the night he first saw her. Even now, the mere mention of her name fired a longing in his blood that he had no right to feel.

He remembered her three-year-old son Pietro, too. The kid's laugh had made Scythe's temples throb with memories he'd thought he left dead and buried behind him more than a decade ago.

"Are she and the boy all right?" There was dread in his throat as he asked it, but his flat tone gave none of it away.

"Yes. For now." Trygg paused. "She's in danger. It's serious as hell this time."

Scythe's grip on his phone tightened. The woman had been through enough troubles already, starting with the unfit Breed male she'd taken as her mate several years ago. Chiara's bastard of a mate, Sal, had turned out to be a gambler and a first-class asshole.

Unable to pay his debts, he'd wound up on the bad side of a criminal kingpin named Vito Massioni. To square up when Massioni came to collect, Sal traded his own sister, Arabella, in exchange for his life. If not for the Order in Rome—more specifically, one of their warriors, Ettore "Savage" Selvaggio—Bella might still be imprisoned as Massioni's personal pet.

As for Chiara, she was essentially made a captive of Massioni's as well. Sal's treachery hadn't saved him in the end. After his death, Chiara and her son lived at the family vineyard under the constant threat of Massioni's danger.

Six weeks ago, it had all come to a head. The Order had moved in on Massioni, taking out him and his operation... or so they'd thought. Massioni had survived the explosion that obliterated his mansion and all of his lieutenants, and he was out for blood.

Chiara and her son had ended up in the crosshairs along with Bella and Savage, putting all of them on the run. Trygg sent them to Scythe for shelter, knowing damned well that Scythe wasn't in the habit of playing protector to anyone. Least of all a woman and child.

And he still wasn't in that habit now.

Nevertheless, the question rolled off his tongue too easily. "Tell me what happened."

"According to Bella, Chiara's had the sensation she was being watched for the past week or so. Stalked from afar. Last night, things took a turn for the worst. A Breed male broke into the villa. If she hadn't heard him outside her window and had time to prepare, she'd likely have been raped, murdered, or both."

"Motherfu—" Scythe bit off the curse and took a steadying breath. His rage was on full boil, but he rallied his thoughts around gathering facts. "Did the son of a bitch touch her? How did she manage to get away?"

"Sal kept a sword hidden beneath the bed in case Massioni ever sent some muscle there to work him over for the money he owed. After he died, Chiara left the weapon in place. By some miracle of adrenaline or determination, she was able to fight the bastard off, but barely."

Holy hell. As he thought of the tiny slip of a woman trying to fight off a healthy Breed male he shook his head slowly in disbelief. The fact that she survived was beyond lucky or even miraculous, but Trygg was right. The odds of her doing it again were slim to none.

Which was, apparently, where Scythe and his specific set of skills came in. Not that it would take a request from Trygg or the Order to convince him to hunt down Chiara's attacker and make the Breed male pay in blood and anguish.

The very idea of her cowering as some animal attempted to harm her made Scythe's whole body quake with fiery rage.

"So, the Order needs me to find this bastard and tear

his head off, then?"

"Just killing him isn't going to get to the root of the problem. We don't think this attack is random. The Order needs you to protect Chiara and Pietro while we work to figure out who's after her and why."

Scythe could not hold back the snarl that built in his throat. "You know I don't do bodyguard duty. Damn it, you know why too."

"Yeah," Trygg said. "And I'm still asking you to do it. You're the only one we can trust with this, brother. The Order's got all hands on deck with Opus Nostrum, Rogue outbreaks, and ninety-nine other problems at the moment. We need you."

Scythe groaned. "You ask too fucking much this time."

Protecting the woman would cost him. He knew that from both instinct and experience. For almost a score, he'd kept his feedings down to once a week. His body's other needs were kept on an even tighter leash.

He'd only spent a few hours with Chiara Genova six weeks ago, yet it was long enough to know that being under the same roof with her was going to test both his patience and his self-discipline.

But the kid? That was a no-go. There were things he just couldn't do, not even for his brother.

He mulled over Trygg's request in miserable silence.

"What's it gonna be, Scythe?"

The refusal sat on the tip of his tongue, but damned if he could spit it out. "If I do this, we do it my way. I don't answer to the Order or to anyone else. Agreed?"

"Sure, you got it. Just get your ass to Rome as soon as you can so we can go over your plan and coordinate efforts."

11

"What about her?" Scythe demanded. "Does Chiara know you've contacted me to help her?"

The stretch of silence on the other end of the line told him all he needed to know and he grimaced.

"Savage and Bella are bringing Chiara and Pietro in as we speak," Trygg said. "They should all be here within the hour."

Scythe cursed again, more vividly this time. "I'm on my way."

He ended the call, then threw the SUV into gear and gunned it out to the street.

CHAPTER 2

"**A**bsolutely not. It's out of the question."

Chiara crossed her arms over her chest and glared at the assembled warriors as if they'd lost their minds. They must have, if they thought she would agree to anything they'd just explained.

"I'm not leaving Rome without my son. I haven't been apart from Pietro for more than a few hours since he was born. You think I'm going to start now, when you suspect some animal is out to kill me?"

She shook her head furiously, pacing the conference room in agitation. She'd agreed to keep an open mind when Ettore and Bella brought her to the Order's command center earlier tonight, but that didn't mean she was going to let them separate her from her boy.

She turned to face her former sister-in-law, desperate for an ally.

"Bella, please. You know I'd do just about anything you asked. When you and Ettore took Pietro and me from the vineyard to keep us safe from Vito Massioni and his men, I went without argument. But this? There has to be another way."

No one answered, just as no one had answered any of her other questions and protests, either. She caught the subtle shift of Ettore's gaze toward the far side of the meeting room where a Breed male who wasn't part of the Order stood. He wasn't a stranger to her, although she could hardly claim to be completely comfortable in his presence, despite the fact that some weeks ago she and Pietro had taken shelter in his safe house in Matera along with Bella and Ettore.

Tall and broad, immense even for a Gen One, as he was, Scythe was a wall of muscle and menace. His all-black clothing was a sinister complement to his long ebony hair and close-trimmed beard. Even his eyes were black. His intelligent, unreadable obsidian gaze seemed to see everything, know everything.

Chiara had been trying to ignore Scythe's unsettling presence ever since he arrived.

Impossible.

Not only because he was the kind of male who seemed to swallow up every bit of oxygen in the room, but because she had only moments ago been informed that he would be responsible for protecting her life.

He didn't seem any happier about that idea than she was.

She could feel the weight of his cold obsidian gaze on her face, but she couldn't bring herself to look in his direction. She knew she was being stubborn, but dammit, Pietro was all she had.

More importantly, she was all he had too. They were a little family of two. Asking her to let him out of her sight in this situation was like asking her to hand over her beating heart in a basket.

"What if I took Pietro out of Italy instead? We can go to America for a while. We can hide somewhere together for as long as the Order needs us to. Anything but separating me from my child."

If she'd hoped to get some vocal support from Bella, she'd been sorely disappointed. The room filled with a tense silence and Chiara's nerves felt stretched and raw. She drifted over to the bar cart in the corner and poured herself a brandy from a crystal decanter.

Her mind grappled for some other argument, no matter how thin. Anything to keep her son close.

"The boy will be safer away from you, Chiara."

It was Scythe's deep voice that finally broke the silence, the first thing he'd said to her all night. She wheeled on him, her pulse pounding with unchecked fury at both his words and his uncanny ability to read her like a book. "Easy for you to say. How many children do you have?"

His hard gaze drilled into her for a long moment before he shook his head. "I have none."

"Then how could you possibly understand the magnitude of what you're asking?" Her voice was trembling now, and she hated herself for it, but it couldn't be helped. "What kind of mother ships her child off for someone else to care for when there is danger near?"

Just the thought of it made her skin break out in a cold sweat.

But the Hunter wasn't giving up so easily. "A good mother. If the choice is keeping him close so you can be together when you die or letting him go and giving him his best chance of survival, you'd be foolish to consider the former. And selfish."

He stepped away from his assumed post next to the door and moved into the center of the room. The space seemed to shrink with every step he took. By the time his long, muscled legs had brought him to within arm's reach of her she was almost claustrophobic with the overwhelming size and power that emanated from him. He towered over her, his trim-bearded jaw set in a tight scowl.

"We know one thing. If this male truly wanted to kill you, he would have. Instead, when you fought back, he chose to retreat. He evidently wants you alive, and I'm guessing that's because he wants you for his own."

Dear God, she tried not to flinch at the idea, but the prospect of being taken by her attacker—or worse, shackled by a forced blood bond she would be powerless to break except in death—made her heart lurch in her breast.

Scythe's voice took on a sober tone, but it was far from merciful. "Make no mistake, Chiara. Males who would stalk and mate without your consent are no better than animals. He won't want to share you with anyone, least of all a man-child you love with such deep devotion. The first thing he'll do once he has you is kill Pietro. I guarantee it."

A ragged cry erupted from her throat and she held a hand to her mouth in horror.

Scythe's dark brow furrowed into a scowl. "I know it's hard to hear, but the safest place for your boy is wherever you aren't."

He was right. She knew it the second he'd spoken the words, but God. How could she bear being away from her son?

He'd already suffered so much in his very young life.

"If you agree to follow my instructions in this, I promise you'll be reunited with Pietro soon. I'll stake my own life on that."

She glanced at the others in the room, desperate for alternatives, yet knowing in her gut that she had to do what was best for her son. Even if it meant leaving Rome without him and putting her life in the hands of her unwanted guardian.

"If I have to protect you both," Scythe muttered, "my attention will be split and neither of you will be truly safe."

Arguing was futile at this point, and she knew it. Her only hope was that Scythe would keep his word and do his best to catch her assailant as quickly as possible. Then maybe she and Pietro could get back to the work of trying to have some semblance of a normal life.

She lifted the snifter to her lips in a trembling hand and took a long sip, relishing the heat blazing a path to her belly.

"All right. I'll do as you ask. But not if it means I need to live like a prisoner at your place in Matera with nothing for me to do except worry about my child. I want to go home to the vineyard, so I can at least work and keep my hands and mind busy while you and the Order do whatever it is you need to do."

To her shock, Scythe gave an agreeing nod. "That is the plan, actually. It will be best if things appear as normal as possible. We want this male to be tempted to make another move. We want to lure him in as quickly as possible."

"Encourage him to attack again?" She found it

difficult to keep the nervous edge from her voice.

"You couldn't be safer," Trygg interjected, the grim male nodding in Scythe's direction. "My brother has the ability to sense imminent danger, so he'll be waiting for your assailant the whole time. He's also got the lethal skills to take the bastard out in a hundred different ways."

Chiara swallowed, loath to imagine just how deadly a massive Gen One Breed and former Hunter like Scythe could be—despite that he was missing one hand.

Bella stepped forward and offered her a reassuring touch. "Ensuring that you and Pietro are safe is the most important thing, *sorella*."

"Yes," Ettore agreed. "And that means we can't simply hide you both away and hope that whoever attacked you decides to give up. We need to know who he is, and what he wants. We need to be sure we cut this threat off at the root."

"And we will," said the third member of the Order's Rome team, their dark-haired commander, Lazaro Archer. "While you are under Scythe's watch, my team will be working on leads in the background. If things go well, this could all be over in the next few days."

Chiara glanced at the Breed elder. "And if it doesn't go well?"

Lazaro gave her a grim look. "Follow Scythe's instructions and I have no doubt that you and your son will both be fine. Leave the rest to the Order."

So, she was essentially going to be putting herself under the yoke of an overbearing, clearly dangerous male she hardly knew and setting herself up as bait for her stalker as well. Could this situation possibly get any worse?

The answer was yes, because no matter how uncomfortable she was with the plan that had just been described to her, it would be unbearable if it meant putting Pietro at risk along with her.

As much as she bristled against the idea of being separated from her son, she knew what Scythe said was true. It would be foolish—even selfish—to insist on keeping Pietro with her.

She exhaled a shaky breath. "I will do this, but you need to let me explain this to Pietro myself. He's not going to understand it all, but he needs to hear it from me that I'm only leaving for a little while, and because I have no other choice."

Already, her heart gave a squeeze as she pictured his big, dark eyes filled with confusion.

"You can tell him now," Scythe said, waving her on with his left hand. "We'll be leaving in five minutes."

Her mouth swung open as she stared at him, incredulous. "So soon? I'll need more time than that to say goodbye to my child."

"Ten minutes, then. No more."

He said it with an unyielding tone that set her teeth on edge. Was he so eager to have her under his heel that he intended to start pushing her around before they'd even left the room?

Maybe the old Chiara would have fallen in line without a squeak of resistance. The naive Chiara who had allowed herself to be swept into Sal's lies and deceit, never seeing her mate for what he truly was until she found herself bonded to him by blood. The sheltered Chiara whose lack of a backbone had nearly cost her son his life six weeks ago when Vito Massioni came to kill them all.

The old Chiara was dead now. A stronger woman had emerged from that ordeal. And the second they were alone, she was going to explain that to Scythe.

She set her glass down on the bar with a clink and shuffled past Scythe, ignoring the heat that shot through her as her breasts brushed his chest.

Jesus, could he take up any more *space?*

He followed her into the hallway, his long strides easily keeping pace with her as she walked to the room where Bella and Ettore had taken Pietro when Scythe arrived a short while ago.

Through the glass in the corridor, she watched her son flip through the pages of a picture book he held in his little lap. Although he was Breed, like his father, and would one day grow up to be as formidable as any of his kind, right now Pietro was simply a little boy. Her precious, cherished child.

The thought of leaving him raked at her and she pivoted a hard look at Scythe at her back. "I'll let you know when I'm ready to go."

She started to reach for the door and was shocked to feel his fingers clamp down around her wrist. Shocked, not because she found his touch offensive, but because of the jolt of heat—of pure, sensual awareness—that brief connection sent through her body.

"Ten minutes, Chiara." His black eyes crackled with sparks of amber as he glowered down at her. "It's important that your assailant doesn't suspect you've been shaken enough to go for help. We need to be back at the vineyard as soon as possible."

She swallowed and took a step away from him, away from the heat his big body was generating.

Before she could open the door, Pietro was racing

toward it on his own, having spotted her through the window.

"Mama!" he cried as she stepped inside with him, his chubby cheeks stretching into a dimpled smile. He held out his picture book, practically shoving it into her hands. "Read to me, Mama?"

She swallowed hard to dislodge the knot in her throat and forced a grin in return. "Okay, but only a few pages, sweetheart. Maybe we can get Aunt Bella to read to you when I'm done. Would you like that?"

He nodded enthusiastically before plopping down on the floor and tugging her beside him. Even at three years old, he had the strength of a child more than twice his age. But his face was pure innocence as he stared up at her and urged her to begin reading.

She settled him onto her lap and began reciting the words on the page.

She sensed Scythe there long before his shadow eclipsed her, but she resisted the urge to wheel around and order him out of the room. Pietro was so sensitive and sharp. All of them needed to show a united front or he would sense something was amiss. The last thing she wanted was for him to be fearful.

"You remember Scythe, don't you?"

"Uh-huh," Pietro said, turning his cherubic face toward the Breed male. A smile lit her son's face as he stared up at the forbidding Hunter who was a nightmare in black from his long ebony hair and the trimmed, dark beard that clung to his squared jaw and gave him a sinister edge, to the leather duster and heavy combat boots on his monstrous feet. "Hi, Scythe!"

He nodded at the boy, but his gaze was filled with warning as he glanced at Chiara.

"What're you doing here, Scythe?" Pietro asked innocently.

Chiara cleared her throat. Before her grim companion offered an answer that might terrify her son, she hurried to explain what was happening. "Mama has to go back to the vineyard tonight, so Scythe is going to take me there."

"You're going home?" Pietro's face scrunched in confusion.

"Just for a few days, sweetheart."

"Me too?"

"No, baby. Just Mama." She smoothed her hand over his silken dark hair that was the same chocolate shade as her own. "I need you to stay here and keep Aunt Bella company for me. Can you do that?"

He nodded. "I like Aunt Bella. She gave me this book, and Uncle Ettore said he was gonna let me play that game with the cars that go really fast and crash into things."

Chiara's brows arched. "Did he now?"

At that same moment, Bella and Ettore both entered the room. Bella's mate had the good grace to offer a sheepish shrug as Pietro launched himself out of Chiara's arms and ran to embrace the Breed warrior.

Ettore ruffled the boy's hair. "Easy there, champ. You're gonna get me in trouble with your mom. That game was going to be our little secret, remember?"

Pietro's eyes narrowed and he shut his mouth, locking it tight with an invisible key.

Chiara rolled her eyes. "Nice," she murmured, but the fact was, she couldn't be too angry.

Pietro was enjoying his visit here tonight, and there was no question that he was in good hands. In fact, visits from Bella and Ettore were one of the few spots of normal in her son's life, and she wasn't about to begrudge any of them that. She certainly didn't have to worry about Pietro feeling abandoned. If anything, he was excited.

"We should go."

Scythe's grave murmur sliced through the lightness of the moment. And now seemed as good a time as any for her to muster the strength to hug her son and say goodbye.

Through sheer force of will, she managed to hold back her tears as she held him close and whispered that she loved him, that she would be back to collect him before he had time to miss her.

She hoped her promise wasn't an empty one.

The only thing standing between her vow to return to her son and the unknown that waited for her back at the vineyard was the hulking wall of menace who loomed in silence now at the door.

Chiara released Pietro and allowed herself to be folded into the warm embrace of Bella's arms.

"He'll be just fine, *sorella*. And so will you. Scythe will see to that."

Chiara nodded, steeling herself for one final glance at her son. Ettore nodded to her in reassurance as Pietro went back to his picture book, innocently unaware of the adult concern that vibrated in the room.

She inhaled sharply, rallying herself for what lay ahead. She could do this. For her son's future and her own, she could face anything.

Even Scythe.

"All right," she murmured, moving toward the door. Tears welled in her eyes, but she refused to let them fall.

Not in front of her child. And not in front of her emotionless guardian. "Let's go, then."

His fathomless, onyx eyes drilled into hers and, for a second, she caught a glimpse of a pain so stark, so deep, it sent a chill through her. But before she could think on it for too long, it was gone, leaving a shuttered, blank expression in its place.

"Right," he said tonelessly, motioning her into the hallway. "The sooner we get this over with, the sooner we can both go back to our lives."

CHAPTER 3

It was long past midnight by the time Scythe pulled into the vineyard's twisting driveway at the base of Mount Vulture. After several hours behind the wheel, he was twitchy with the need for freedom. He'd elected to take Chiara's Fiat instead of his SUV in the hopes of avoiding notice on the road, a decision he'd regretted more and more with each passing mile. At six-foot-six, his head grazed the ceiling of the tiny vehicle and he had to spread his legs wide in order to accommodate the steering wheel between them.

He felt like a bear trapped in a chicken coop.

Even worse than the discomfort of his cramped muscles was the distraction of Chiara's close proximity in the tight quarters of the car. He could smell the citrusy freshness of her skin and hair, could feel the warmth of her body seated beside him. He could hear the shallow rhythm of her breathing as the silence stretched out between them, could almost feel frantic beating of her heart like a vibration in his own veins.

She stirred other parts of him too. For a Hunter who'd been ruthlessly trained to deny his own wants and needs in favor of duty and self-control, his road trip with Chiara had been a startling reminder of the fact that beneath it all, he was still, ultimately, a flesh-and-blood male. A male who couldn't ignore the soft, beautiful female confined in the small space along with him, no matter how hard he tried.

Even now, his cock rested heavily between his thighs, a throbbing, heated reminder of just how long he'd gone without slaking that other hunger. Under his clothing, the Breed *dermaglyphs* that tracked all over his skin felt tingly and alive, no doubt infusing with all of the deep, changeable colors of his desire. He swallowed on an arid throat and his tongue grazed over the tips of his emerging fangs.

Damn, this wasn't good.

Although he wanted to blame his awareness of Chiara on simple, unchecked lust, the truth was he couldn't recall the last time his body had challenged his iron-hewn will.

Then again, yes he could.

It was only six weeks ago. Back in Matera, when he'd first laid eyes on Chiara Genova.

"Fuck."

She glanced at him, frowning. He didn't have to wonder if she saw the flecks of amber glowing in the blackness of his irises. Her swift intake of breath told him so.

Hopefully she'd assume the sparks were due to irritation, rather than desire. Both emotions were riding him in equal measure, after all.

"Something wrong, Scythe?"

"Yeah. If this winds up taking longer than a couple of days, we're going to need to talk about another mode of transportation."

"You're the one who suggested we take my car," she reminded him.

There was a note to her voice he hadn't heard before and he swiveled a questioning look at her. In the thin light of the dashboard, he saw that her lips were twitching. With a start, he realized that she was struggling not to laugh at him. He had only thought about how uncomfortable it was, but he had to imagine he looked as ridiculous as he felt.

He scowled at her, but his heart wasn't in it.

"I'm sorry," she said, a giggle slipping past her lips. "I really shouldn't laugh. It's just... I'm sorry, it's really not funny. It's just that you're so big and this car is so small. You look like you're driving a dollhouse car. I don't know how you've managed to make this whole trip without getting a nasty Charlie horse in your thigh."

Jesus Christ.

Didn't she realize? A Charlie horse was the least of his discomforts.

He stared at her as she struggled to keep the humor out of her expression. Tried and failed, that is. Another laugh burst out of her. She waved her hand in front of her face as if in apology, but it was no use. Her laughter filled the car, and as prickly and on edge as he felt, he took a strange comfort in the sound.

It was as if a valve had been opened and all of the weight of what had happened—the grim reality of why they both were seated in this vehicle together in the first place—released with each soft giggle that rolled off

Chiara's tongue.

"Are you finished?" he asked, feeling less impatient than his gruff voice suggested.

Deep down, though, he was relieved. Hearing about her harrowing ordeal had him on the razor's edge, too, and filled with a fury that he couldn't justify, but couldn't deny. Her distress at leaving Pietro was almost palpable, and if his discomfort behind the wheel of her miniature vehicle made her forget about all of that for even an instant, he should be thankful.

Having her at ease would make his job all the simpler. She would be more amenable to his instructions, more trusting of him. Less likely to question or challenge his commands when her life depended on letting him handle the lethal business he was born and bred to do.

He doused the headlights as he drove the car up the drive, parking beside the villa and killing the engine. "Stay here. I need to check the perimeter of the house and inside. Once it's clear, I'll come back for you."

She shook her head and started to open her mouth, but he held up his hand to silence her.

"You will follow my orders without questions or argument. That was our agreement, remember?"

"I wasn't going to argue," she replied stiffly, the grin that had been tugging at her lips just a moment before fading away like the sun at dusk. "I was just going to tell you that I had an alarm system installed in the villa a few weeks ago. In order to disarm it, you have to enter the code. Five, seven, seven, eight."

Right.

He handed her the car keys, making sure not to touch her when he did. If he made physical contact with her after the torturous drive, or while the sweet scent of her still clung to his senses and the bright sound of her laughter was still echoing in his ears, he was liable to lose his mind.

Or worse, give in to the hunger she awakened in him.

Alone in his dark den of solitude, it was easier to ignore the pull of the flesh. Here with a beautiful, unmated female so close, he was playing with fire. And Chiara Genova made him want to burn.

Not good at all.

"Slide over to the driver's side and lock the door when I leave," he commanded in a brusque voice. "If I'm not back in five minutes, don't come inside. Start the car and drive away as fast as you can. Head straight back to the Order headquarters. Understand?"

"Scythe, if you think I would turn around and leave you here by your—"

"Damn it, woman." His frustration exploded out of him, motivated chiefly by concern for her. "Just tell me you'll fucking do what I say."

She drew back, her cheeks going pale at his sharp rebuke. "All right, Scythe. I will. I'll stay until you come for me."

There was a spark of indignation, even defiance, in her wide brown eyes, but he didn't have time to test her. Nor did he have the time—or the skills—to try to soothe her. He had a job to do, and the less he had to worry about ruffling her feathers or calming her afterward, the better things would be for both of them.

Regardless of that, he dug deep and called up an image of young Pietro to remind himself of exactly what was at stake here for both of them. Of course, things were tense. It was a life or death situation and she was now separated from her child for the first time. Even Scythe had to admit she was handling it better than he'd expected.

"Five minutes, Chiara. If I don't return by then, leave and don't look back."

He exited the car, sniffing the night air for signs of trouble. So far, his danger antenna was still, and he didn't detect anything out of the ordinary. Fertile, rich soil, the sharp scent of fermentation, sugary grapes and the luscious sweetness of Chiara's skin permeated his senses and he blocked it out with a muttered oath.

He moved stealthily around the back of the sprawling villa to the door that opened into the kitchen. The locks turned free under the power of his mind, then he opened the door and entered on silent feet. No need for Chiara's alarm code; he disabled the flashing sensors with a flick of his thoughts as he stepped farther inside the darkened house.

No signs of trouble as he gazed around the kitchen and into the great room. The place was quiet, no one here now and no evidence that anyone had been there in the time since Chiara had left earlier tonight. The sense of malevolence Scythe would have felt if there was a threat of imminent danger inside the villa was notably absent.

Although he trusted his innate ability, he still made a quick sweep of every room and every point of entry. When it came to keeping Chiara safe, he was leaving nothing left to chance.

Each second she was unprotected and out of his sight as he searched the house felt like an hour. He couldn't deny the relief that washed over him when he returned to the car where she waited and found her sitting there, just as he'd instructed, safe and sound behind the wheel.

"All clear," he murmured, as he opened the driver's side door and helped her out.

She met his gaze with a disgruntled glance, then followed him back to the villa in chilly silence. When she reached for the light switch near the kitchen door, Scythe caught her hand and stilled it.

"No lights for now. It's the middle of the night, and we don't want this place lit up like a beacon if anyone's watching. It was risk enough driving up here together at this late hour."

She nodded, slowly withdrawing her fingers from his loose grasp. The warmth of her skin lingered against his palm, sending heat licking up his arm, through his veins... into the distracting thickness at his groin.

"Go on," he commanded her curtly. "Get settled and try to rest. I'll handle things on my end. I need to get the tactical equipment from the car, and I plan to set up some surveillance points around the property before sunrise."

She nodded, but remained standing in front of him. Too damned close for his peace of mind. "There's a small guest room down the hall from the master bedroom. I didn't know to prepare it for you ahead of time, but it'll only take me a few minutes to—"

"No." His sharp reply cut her off. "I won't be sleeping more than a few minutes at a time while I'm on this assignment, and I sure as hell don't plan to get comfortable in a bed."

Least of all in one just steps away from hers.

"Fine." Her lips pressed flat as she stared up at him. "I was only trying to help."

"Don't bother," he snapped. "I can take care of myself. I've been doing it for a long time."

Finally, she retreated, moving back a step. He almost breathed a sigh of relief that she was going—but then instead of pivoting away, she crossed her arms over her breasts and advanced on him, pinning him with a glare.

"Is this how you treat everyone who tries to show you a little kindness? I know I agreed to do what you asked while you're here, but do you plan to scowl and bark orders at me the whole time?"

He scrubbed his hand over his face in frustration. What had happened to the Chiara he'd met six weeks ago in Matera? While he wouldn't have described her as meek, he hadn't seen this kind of fire in her then. That Chiara had seemed so vulnerable. Fragile with fear and uncertainty.

Sure, he had admired her obvious devotion to her son, and he'd seen the kindness that radiated from her. He had appreciated her beauty more than he had a right to—that part of her had been impossible to ignore or to forget in all the time since. How many times had he been tempted to venture out to Potenza just for another glimpse of her? How many times had he woken from fevered dreams where he had Chiara naked in his arms, moaning in pleasure?

Christ, too many to count. But he'd resisted, knowing a delicate female like Chiara would crumble in his ungentle hands like a dried rose petal.

This woman before him, her warm brown eyes flashing, pert breasts heaving with her indignation, was someone else entirely. And damned if he didn't want this new Chiara even more.

He'd been brought in to protect her, yet all he could

think about right now was how sweet she must taste. Not what he'd come here to do.

She took his silence as an opportunity to press further.

"I don't know why you agreed to watch over me when it's obvious you'd rather be doing anything else. But like it or not, it appears we're stuck with each other for the time being."

"Yes, we are," he agreed. "So, do us both a favor and try to pretend I'm not here."

She balked. "You can't be serious. When's the last time you looked in a mirror? You're not exactly easy to miss."

Neither was she, and he realized the idiocy of his suggestion as soon as he said it. Still, he hoped his gruffness would push her away, if only for his peace of mind. He had numerous things to do yet tonight and arguing with Chiara wasn't going to get any of them done.

All it was doing was making him twitchy with the need to silence her, even if he had to do it with his own mouth on hers.

"I'm not going to walk around on eggshells in my own home, Scythe. And no matter what you say, I'm not going to forget for a second why you're here. My life is in your hands. Do you think that means nothing to me?" She expelled a short laugh. "While we're on the subject, did you actually think I would've driven off and left you here to die alone if there had been trouble when we arrived?"

Yes, he had. He'd more than thought it, he'd expected her to follow his instructions to the letter. "I wouldn't have died, Chiara. I've gone up against a dozen

Breed males at a time and walked away the only one still breathing. Your stalker won't be any match for me. Killing is what I was born to do."

It took her a moment to absorb that. "Well, either way, I wouldn't have left. What kind of person do you imagine I am?"

He knew she didn't expect him to answer, so he didn't voice any of the replies that popped into his mind.

A foolish one.

A stubborn one.

A beautiful one.

A brave one.

"I may not have asked you to play my protector, Scythe, but I am grateful to have you."

She edged closer, leaving him no option but to hold his ground or back away from her advance. He chose the former, even though every instinct in his body warned him it was a mistake to let her any nearer.

"And I'm grateful for how you sheltered Pietro and me along with Bella and Ettore when we came to you in Matera too. Maybe none of that means anything to you, but it does to me. So you'll just have to forgive me for trying to be nice or hospitable to you."

A tendon pulsed in his jaw as he stared down at her. This was dangerous territory, allowing her to think of him as some sort of savior. Dangerous for him, and for her.

Rather than succumb to the urge to touch her, his left hand flexed and fisted at his side, while the stump on his right wrist throbbed in useless stillness.

It wasn't hard to recall the mistake that had cost him his other hand. He'd let his guard down once, had let emotion cloud his reason and paid a steep price for it.

Not only him, but two other people he cared for.

Never again.

That lesson—that awful regret—would stay with him forever.

"I have no need for soft words or tender concern," he told her, praying she would heed it as the warning he intended. "Don't expect me to provide those things to you, either. That's not who I am. Look at me only as a weapon. A deadly one you'd be wise to steer clear of until this whole thing is over."

She didn't cower, even though he'd made grown Breed males tremble with less venom than he showed her now. She drew her shoulders more squarely, her eyes narrowed as she slowly shook her head.

"You're not a weapon, Scythe. You're flesh and blood. You're a man."

"I am a Hunter," he corrected her. "That's what I was born. That's how I live. It's how, eventually, I expect I will die."

As he spoke, he watched her gaze flick away from his face, drifting lower. Her eyes paused on the web of scars that ringed his neck where his collar used to be. The ultraviolet-powered tether he'd been forced to wear had ensured he and the rest of his Hunter brethren obeyed their Master without fail.

It had been two decades since the Order's victory over his creator had freed him and the rest of his Gen One half-brothers from the hellish program, but there were times when Scythe still felt the cold, unbreakable black cuff around his throat.

Times like now, when Chiara's tender gaze seemed riveted on the scars left behind from his enslavement.

"Dragos did all of this to you?"

Hearing the villain's name on her tongue made his gut twist. He didn't want to imagine she knew anything of the horrors Dragos and his followers had perpetrated before the Order had finally wiped the lot of them from the earth. God knew he didn't want her pity. He would rather walk into full sunlight than face that from her.

"Don't let my scars fool you. I earned every one of them. Dragos may have shackled my body, but he never broke my will."

She said nothing, merely continued to stare at his neck, and at the bared wedge of his chest that peeked out from the unbuttoned collar of his black shirt.

Even worse, she reached up without warning and touched the ruined skin at the base of his throat. The unexpected brush of her fingertips took him completely aback. So much so, he lost all capacity for words or motion.

Locked in place where he stood, he stared wildly, helplessly, as she traced the ropy welt from one side of his neck to the other. He sucked in a sharp breath at her touch, holding stock-still as she traced the patchwork of scars. She continued her journey all the way around to the back, until her fingers brushed the long hair at his nape.

Her delicate exploration of him sent a shaft of white-hot need arcing through him so strongly, it made his hunger to feed the night before pale in comparison. His fangs punched from his gums. His *dermaglyphs* writhed, heating beneath his clothing, his arousal intensifying with each passing second.

Her attention—and the swift physical reaction it stoked in him—was too much to bear. He wheeled back on a low, harsh curse.

"Oh, God. I'm sorry." She blinked as if suddenly shaken from an impulse she'd had no ability to control. Her hand cradled against her chest, she took a step away from him. Then another. "Scythe, forgive me. I—"

"Forget it," he snarled, although the gravel in his voice had less to do with anger than with the hard pound of blood rushing through his veins. His cock pressed against the zipper of his black jeans, having gone as hard as stone long before she'd been so foolish as to touch him.

He stared down at her, at a loss as to how to proceed. So far, she'd either shocked or defied him at every turn, neither of which he could allow. If he was to keep her safe, he needed to maintain a strict control.

Running roughshod over her hadn't worked, and God knew he had no idea how to navigate around other people. He was accustomed to working alone, being alone. Concerning himself with another person's feelings and emotions—especially a woman's—wasn't anything he'd needed to practice in years.

Not since Mayrene.

The thought of her sent a shaft of pain through him and he steeled himself against it, blocking the weakness of his emotion as he'd been so expertly trained to do. Thinking of the other time he'd tried, and failed, to protect someone would do him no good here.

He wasn't going to fail Chiara.

He would die before he had to live through another loss like that.

Scythe raked his hand over his scalp on a low curse. "Sunrise will be here soon. Go to bed, Chiara. I'll secure the premises and begin my watch."

She nodded, still backing away from him as if she'd

just been burned.

He kept his gaze locked on the wall so as not to stare at the gentle sway of her hips as she finally turned around and left the kitchen. His cock was still throbbing from the touch of her fingers on his skin, and the last thing he needed was more reason to regret pushing her away.

He clutched the car keys in his hand and headed back outside, his mood getting blacker by the moment.

To think he'd considered Pietro to be the bigger distraction to his mission. He'd been so concerned about a child's presence wreaking havoc on his mental state that he'd completely underestimated how thoroughly Chiara might distract him. Even now, she was out of sight, but he felt her presence burrowing deeper and deeper into his senses.

Stalking out to the vehicle, Scythe grabbed his gear and set about preparing for his task at hand. As relieved as he was to know that Chiara was safe and sound under his watch now, a part of him yearned for her attacker to make his move—and soon.

Because the faster he could finish this assignment, the faster he could move on and try to put Chiara Genova out of his mind.

His plan for the remainder of the night entailed constructing a strong defense. Then it would end with a call to the Order in Rome to ensure that they were working on a plan for the offense as well.

And when this ordeal was all over? Brethren or not, Scythe was going to tell Trygg to do him a favor and lose his fucking number.

CHAPTER 4

Chiara swiped a hand over her sweaty forehead and looked up into the late afternoon sky with a sigh of relief. The faint pulling sensation in her lower back was almost welcome. It meant that she'd done a hard day's work, and just maybe she'd get some sleep tonight.

She'd needed the physical outlet and time in the sun so badly. Thankfully, Scythe hadn't fought her too hard on it, if only because the daylight was a guaranteed protection against any Breed with designs on harming her.

Nevertheless, she'd felt Scythe's constant gaze on her from inside the villa all day—courtesy of the network of hidden motion sensors he'd placed all around the property while she'd slept last night. Or tried to sleep, at any rate.

She thought back to the night before and winced, her cheeks heating with embarrassment.

Oh, my God.

What kind of lunatic just started touching a man like she had last night? Especially a man she hardly knew.

But something had taken hold of her as they'd faced off in her kitchen, and it wasn't until she'd noticed the *glyphs* at the top of his chest changing color that she realized she had acted on her impulse to touch him. The intense curiosity—and, yes, the irresistible desire—to explore all those hard edges and battle scars had overwhelmed all of her good sense. To say nothing of her propriety.

Not that Scythe seemed to be the kind of male who knew anything about that.

How had he come to be the man he was? Rude. Arrogant, for sure. But wounded and dark too. As much as he had tried to convince her otherwise, there was an integrity about him. A sense of honor that she doubted he let many people see. She had witnessed it in the way he'd treated Pietro back in Matera, then again in Rome last night.

He had denied that he had any kindness in him last night, but she had seen him treat her son gently. He'd been kind to her before too.

Before she'd started pawing him like a lovesick fool.

God, what he must think of her.

She hitched the shovel off her shoulder and plunged it into the soft earth with a groan. Of all the times she wished she'd had the Breed power to wipe her own memory, it was now.

Once she'd gone to bed last night, things hadn't been much better. She was alone, separated from Scythe by two doors and a long, sweeping hallway, but his presence was everywhere, leaving no corner of her home, life, or mind untouched. And when she finally drifted off to sleep, even her dreams had betrayed her.

She'd woken up hot and aching and full of longing she hadn't felt since... well, ever.

She swallowed hard as her nipples peaked beneath her thin cotton shirt. This was all some hard-wired, primal response to how starkly different Scythe was than her deceased husband.

Sal had been handsome and charming, but he'd also been mentally weak and ineffectual. A coward who cared for himself more than he had ever cared for others. Her foolish, blind love for him had nearly cost both her own life and the life of their son. It stood to reason that she would instinctively be attracted to someone who was the exact opposite of him.

And there was no one more opposite from charming, oily Sal than forbidding, prickly Scythe.

She squeezed her eyes closed and allowed herself to picture him one more time. The hard, unforgiving lines of his face, only more sculpted by the black beard he kept trimmed close to his square-cut jaw. That firm but slightly full mouth. His massive body, so capable and strong... lethally so.

A shudder went through her, though not from fear. She groaned in frustration, yet unable to purge the image of Scythe from her thoughts. Nor from her overheated senses.

Enough. This soil wasn't going to turn itself.

For the next hour, until the sun started to dip low in the sky, she tended her fields, grateful for the solitude and the distraction of good, hard work. She worked until every muscle screamed in protest and until her skin was damp with a sheen of sweat, despite the chill in the air.

She'd left the house early that morning, after finally

persuading Scythe that she would be safe in the vineyard and needed the physical outlet. He had seemed happy enough to avoid her, busying himself with monitoring his video sensors inside and around the rambling house and fielding calls from Trygg and the Order in Rome.

Now, the sky was changing from blush to dusty purple, and she knew she was going to have to face him soon. There was no chance he'd let her work out here alone once it got dark, no matter how many silent alarms he'd set nor how strong his unique ability to sense danger was.

She had just placed her shovel down and was beginning to pack up her water bottle and supplies when Scythe's low voice sounded from behind her.

"It's getting late."

Her heart pounded as she turned to face him. He stood with his hand on one hip, the other arm hanging loosely at his side. He wore a black T-shirt that bared his *dermaglyph*-covered arms and stretched tight across the wall of muscle that was his chest. Faded jeans rode his hips and long legs, hinting at iron-hewn thighs and a distractingly large bulge at his groin.

Her tongue stuck to the roof of her mouth as she imagined tracing every line. What the hell was wrong with her? Was she so physically deprived after her dead mate's betrayal that she should lose all sense when it came to this male?

Three years in an empty bed hadn't seemed so long until she was standing in front of Scythe.

"It will be dark soon. You shouldn't be out here."

She got to her feet, brushing dirt from her work pants. "I-I was just coming in anyway."

He inclined his head, then shot a glance around the

vineyard, taking in the rows of vibrant, twisting vines and plump grapes. She had weeded several rows today, the turned earth rich and loose now, the color of dark coffee grounds.

"How long have you been doing this by yourself?"

She shrugged. "After Sal was killed and Bella was taken away by Vito Massioni, it was hard to keep a steady crew around here. Most of the workers fled that same night. It's one thing for humans to know they live among vampires, but still another to have them witness the kind of violence that Massioni delivered and expect them not to run far and forever away. I had a handful of loyal employees, but after Massioni sent his thugs here six weeks ago, even they left and never returned."

Scythe grunted, his expression pensive. "It's not sustainable, you know. You'll need help if you mean to keep the vineyard going."

She tucked her gloves into her pocket, bristling at his assessment, even if she knew in her heart that he was right. "I'll manage. I always have."

"Hard life for you here. And for your boy."

"True, but I don't mind working hard. Sometimes I feel like this land saved me. After Sal was gone, it was the only thing I had left besides Pietro. I keep this place going for my son." She let go of a quiet laugh. "And for my own sanity."

Scythe's stare seemed to bore into her as she spoke. She hadn't intended to bare her soul to him, no more than he probably cared to hear about her past mistakes.

She waved her hand dismissively. "I'm rambling. Must be all the sun I had today."

"It takes a strong woman to survive everything you did and come out the other side. Your son is very lucky to have a mother like you."

His words rocked her back on her heels and she met his gaze.

She was gaping, but she couldn't help it. "Was that a compliment?"

She had to struggle to keep a light tone, because if she thought too hard about how deeply she needed to hear reassurance like that, she might crumble.

Yes, definitely too much sun.

It was impacting her vision, too, making her imagine that the odd light in his obsidian gaze might be something tender, something close to admiration.

"It was a compliment, Chiara. One you certainly have earned."

She waited for him to say something more, something critical of her or her stubborn refusal to leave the vineyard after the ordeal with Massioni had ended six weeks ago.

But he didn't.

Scythe's compliment was just that. The praise warmed her even more. It made her realize how accustomed she'd become to Sal's disapproval, to the control he exerted over her in everything she did, and how long she had gone without hearing a simple word of support or encouragement.

Chiara swallowed. "Thank you, Scythe."

He shrugged. "No need for thanks. I only speak the truth."

"Well, I appreciate it. More than you know."

Whether it was the fresh air and sun, Scythe's kindness, or a combination of them all, she found herself admitting something she hadn't acknowledged to anyone before, not even Bella. "There was a time that I felt such crushing guilt over Sal. I mean, how could I not have seen him for what he was? How could I not have known what kind of man he was before I was bound to him as his mate?" She toed a loose clump of dirt and shrugged. "I still struggle with that, with respecting myself. For three years, I've walked around wondering if my instincts are broken or if I'm just blind. But then, when I see Pietro, I remember that I had to be with Sal—no matter what he did or the kind of male he turned out to be. I wouldn't change a thing, because then I wouldn't have that perfect little boy. That probably sounds very stupid to you."

"No." His jaw flexed as he slowly shook his head. "It isn't stupid to love your child. It isn't stupid to sacrifice for him. As for the male you took as your mate..."

When his words trailed off, Chiara couldn't let it go. "Say it."

"It's not my place."

She folded her arms and cocked her head at him. "Look around, Scythe. It's just you and me and acres of grapevines. Tell me what you're thinking."

In the rising dusk, his obsidian irises seemed fathomless, unreadable. Yet deep within the pools of black, embers of orange light flickered. He held her gaze in a way that made her heart flutter in her rib cage and her breath seize in her lungs.

"Sal Genova was a spineless, worthless male. The pain he caused you and your son—the danger he put you both in with his weakness and cowardice—is unthinkable. It's reprehensible. If I had the chance to bring the bastard back to life only to ash him for pleasure, I would do it."

Scythe's voice was almost a growl, unearthly and

lethal. She realized in that instant exactly how dangerous he was. There was no question he meant every word he spoke. And in spite of the fact that those words were bloodthirsty and full of banked rage—in spite of the fact that she could feel menace radiating off his immense body—she felt nothing but a warm sense of relief.

In truth, she felt more than relief.

The heat moved through her like a caress, gathering in the center of her. Scythe would kill for her. That's what he'd come here to do as her protector for the Order, but this admission held far more weight than even that humbling commitment.

She wanted to thank him for what he said, but the air between them had grown intense, vibrating with unspoken awareness. With the attraction that hadn't faded since last night.

She felt it, and there was no mistaking the fact that he did too.

The embers in his eyes smoldered even brighter now, and along the muscles of his bared arms, his *glyphs* pulsed and churned with darkening colors. Indigo, wine, and burnished gold. All the shades of Breed desire.

He parted his lips to let a curse slip off his tongue, and she glimpsed the diamond-bright tips of his fangs.

"Scythe," she whispered, unsure what she wanted to say to him. She reached for him, but he stepped back.

"Inside, Chiara." The command was a rasp, all gravel and gruff impatience. "We've lingered out here longer than we should."

CHAPTER 5

S he was going to be the death of him.

Of all the trials he'd endured, all the torture and the battles that could have—*should have*—taken him down any number of times, this diminutive female was going to be the one to vanquish him if he wasn't careful.

The thought might have amused him if he wasn't in so much agony. Even now as he watched her bustle around the kitchen, freshly showered and dressed in a loose, peach-colored sweater and soft cream leggings, his fangs throbbed in his gums. Ever since he'd seen her out there, working the land, bent over the dirt, beads of sweat glistening on her face and throat, his cock had been hard and aching.

The realization that he was facing another night with her only yards away and nothing but a few paces and a couple of panels of flimsy wood between them made his temples pound and his blood thrum with need.

He should have avoided her after they had come

inside, but part of him needed to be reassured that he could handle being around her without losing his focus. He needed her to know that, too, especially considering how poorly he'd been able to hide his physical reaction to her thus far.

She'd have to be blind or completely naïve to miss how powerfully she affected him. And Chiara was neither of those things.

She was intelligent and observant. He was learning that she was also astonishingly capable and independent, considering how admirably she managed not only her own life and her son's, but the life of the vineyard. Yet she was also soft and gentle, sheltered in ways Scythe didn't think it wise to imagine. The combination was a potent one, particularly when her doe-eyed, dark-haired beauty was temptation enough on its own.

"I spoke to Pietro after I got out of the shower," she said, her voice bright as she plated her meal at the stove. "He couldn't sound happier. Apparently, Bella made him a cape and he's been wearing it constantly, pretending to be a superhero."

She smiled wistfully as she carried her dinner to the table and sat down across from Scythe. "I suppose I should be glad he doesn't understand what's going on. I *am* glad, but I just . . ." She shrugged. "It's been the two of us for so long, it doesn't feel right not having him here with me." She let out a quiet laugh. "Maybe I'm the one who needs the distraction more than him."

Scythe could use a distraction himself, his thoughts still snagged on the uninvited mental image of Chiara emerging wet and naked from her shower. He shifted on the wooden kitchen chair, but it was no use. Nothing was going to make him comfortable.

Nothing except scratching the itch this female had pricked in him since the moment he first laid eyes on her.

Not going to happen.

He shifted again, watching through hooded eyes as she cut a small piece of steak and brought it to her mouth. Her lips closed around the tip of her fork and she sighed as she chewed, pleasure lighting her sun-kissed face.

The groan that was building in his throat must have been audible to her, because she glanced up at him abruptly.

"I got so busy outside today, I forgot to eat lunch," she rushed to explain. "I didn't realize how hungry I was until now."

She set down her fork and took a sip of red wine from an elegant crystal glass. The dark green bottle she'd poured from was unlabeled, the wine's rich bouquet enticing, even to his Breed senses.

"It's one of ours," she said, as he tore his gaze from her and looked for something—anything—else to focus on. "This region's soil is perfect for growing Aglianico grapes, but there's something about our land here that brings out the complexity of the wine."

She took another sip, and when she drew the glass away, a ruby-red droplet clung to her lush lower lip. She caught it with a swipe of her tongue, and it was all Scythe could do not to moan. He clamped his molars tight, no easy thing with his fangs looming behind the grim line of his mouth.

"It's a shame you can't taste this vintage for yourself," Chiara added. "It's so good, it's practically a religious experience."

For fuck's sake. It was bad enough watching her eat and drink, seeing her soft lips and pink tongue moving in ways that made his evidently permanent erection strain with intensifying pressure against his zipper. Hearing her talk about the wine while everything Breed in him was thinking about the way her blood would taste—the way every soft, creamy inch of her would taste—was a disaster waiting to happen.

"How long has it been for you, Scythe?"

"What?" The reply shot out of him, half in confusion, half in bald panic.

"Since you fed."

She went back to work on her steak, slicing a small piece, then wrapping her mouth around it. Holy hell. Each delicate movement of her jaw and throat made arousal wrench tighter.

Chiara swallowed the bite of meat, tilting her head at him as she reached for her wineglass again. "I feel rude eating in front of you, even though none of this is what you'd want."

Christ, if she only knew what he wanted.

She *had* to know. His *glyphs* were pulsing all over his skin, and there was no hiding the glittering flecks of amber that were burning in his eyes.

The fact that she glanced down awkwardly, color flushing her cheeks, told him his body's reaction wasn't going unnoticed.

She placed her fork and knife down on the edge of her plate, then calmly stood up. "Scythe, if you need to feed, then why don't you let me—"

"*No.*" He all but leaped back from the table. Never mind that putting more distance between himself and this luscious female was the last thing his Breed instincts demanded he do. "What the hell are you saying?"

His fangs ached in reflex, his senses going electric in an instant. He reined himself in with a violent curse. Even if he was starved to the brink of death, he wasn't about to entertain the idea of slaking his thirst on Chiara.

If his reasons weren't personal enough, the biggest one of all was the fact that even a taste of Chiara's Breedmate blood would bond him to her for eternity.

And damned if he would ever do that to either one of them.

"Oh." She blanched now, gaping at his furious expression. "You didn't actually think—Oh, God. I was only going to suggest that if you need nourishment, I'm sure that if I called Bella and Ettore, they could arrange to send a blood Host out here for you."

"Forget it." Feeling worse than a bastard and an ass besides, he practically snarled his answer. It took a few moments for his pulse to recover. The rest of him was slower to back down from the jolt of hunger that raked him. "I fed last night, before I arrived in Rome."

He breathed a sigh of relief that he had taken care of that physical need, at least. But the clock was already ticking again, and if his duty for the Order took more than a handful of days, he would have no choice but to seek out fresh red cells.

The thought of feeding at the villa when Chiara was in the same vicinity was nothing he wanted to consider, but leaving her unguarded to hunt for a blood Host away from the vineyard was totally out of the question.

His only hope was to wrap this mission up and get the hell out, the sooner the better.

"Shit." He scrubbed his hand over his bearded jaw. Chiara had gone quiet now, but he could hear the flutter of her pulse beating faster as they both stood facing each other with only the table between them.

He didn't mean to make her uneasy, but his control was being stretched to its limits.

Torture. Every second beside her was sheer agony, and that was coming from a male who had endured heinous, hellish tortures before. More times than he cared to recount.

"Speaking of the Order," he managed through gritted teeth, "I need to check in with Trygg. Will you be all right in here for a few minutes?"

She crossed her arms. "I think I can handle finishing my dinner and cleaning up afterward without supervision."

He frowned at her annoyed tone, but took his opportunity to retreat. It wasn't his custom to flee a difficult situation, but damned if he knew what to do with his disturbing attraction to Chiara.

Tugging his phone from the pocket of his faded jeans, he cut a path toward the open living room just off the kitchen. He was pissed off and unbearably aroused, and it made his voice scrape out of him like razor blades when Trygg answered his call.

"Tell me you have something," he muttered without greeting the other Hunter.

The plan had been that Trygg and the rest of the Order were going to get in touch with a few of their contacts and see if there had been any chatter about other break-ins or attacks in the region.

"Nothing yet," Trygg replied, offering no further comment.

The surly male had never been much for conversation, and until now Scythe had actually appreciated that about him. But with Chiara in the other room and nothing but a long night ahead, Scythe was desperate to kill a little time on safe, solid ground.

"Have you done anything with the description Chiara gave the Order?"

"We ran it through the IID, but there were no hits."

Scythe grunted. The International Identification Database was a relic from the days before First Dawn, back when the Breed was still living in secret from their human neighbors twenty years ago. The registry had been resurrected in recent years, but it was far from complete. Only the most law-abiding civilians in the vampire nation participated in the IID now.

Which left a hell of a lot of room for error.

"So, we can assume the bastard who attacked Chiara probably isn't an upstanding member of Breed society," Scythe drawled. "That leaves a few thousand other options for who we're looking for."

"Tell me something I don't know," Trygg quipped darkly. "We've got other channels open on this. We'll get a lock on this son of a bitch soon."

Scythe swore under his breath. "Do me a favor and make it now."

"Something wrong?" Trygg's reply was toneless, but there was no mistaking the warrior's intensity. "You sensing danger out there already, brother?"

"Yeah. You could say that." Scythe let the answer slide past his teeth and fangs before he could stop it. "It's pushing twenty-four hours and I've got nothing so far. This place is locked down and secure. Not so much as a flicker of trouble tripping my internal radar."

"So, what's the problem?"

It could be summed up in one word, but admitting

LARA ADRIAN

he was allowing himself to get tangled up in his want of the female he'd been sent to protect was a weakness Scythe was not about to expose. Least of all to a male who had endured, and survived, just as much as he had.

Worse, in some ways.

Trygg had eventually found the Order, a fact that Scythe could see had been his brother's saving grace. If barely.

But Scythe had nothing.

He had no one.

Not since Mayrene and her little boy, Jacob.

A human woman and child whom he had once, foolishly, permitted himself to care for as his own.

And, now, here he was, faced with a similar temptation with Chiara.

An even greater temptation, considering she was a Breedmate and letting himself get too close might shackle them both with a bond nothing would sever.

Only death.

He shuddered to consider Chiara's life ending. It wouldn't—not as long as he had breath in his body. But protecting her and wanting her were two different things. One he would give his life for. The other would put both their lives at risk if he didn't find a way to extinguish his impossible desire.

Scythe's grip tightened on his phone. "Just do what you can. Turn over every rock until you find something on this guy and I'll keep things on lockdown over here. I'm going to lose my goddamned mind being forced to lady-sit in the middle of nowhere for nights on end. The faster we can flush the fucker out and drag him in to the Order for questioning, the faster I can get the hell out of here."

He disconnected the call and shoved the phone back into his pocket. As he wheeled around, he found Chiara standing behind him in the arched entry of the kitchen.

The soft light illuminated her from the back, silhouetting her curves and dark, unbound hair in a warm halo.

"Everything all right?"

How long had she been standing there? Had she heard everything he'd just said?

Her schooled expression gave nothing away, but he inwardly kicked himself for not taking more care to make sure he was alone. He'd always been able to rely on his ability to sense danger, so why was it that Chiara never triggered his warning bells until it was too late?

Considering she was literally the most potentially destructive element to his mental well-being in a five-hundred mile radius besides Mount Vesuvius, that was saying something.

"Everything's fine," he uttered sharply. "You should go to bed. I need to go outside and check things, make sure we're secure for the night."

She said nothing, merely gave him a nod then turned and walked away. He stared after her, feeling like a bastard for what he'd said to Trygg, for the fact that she most certainly heard every word.

When she had disappeared into her bedroom and closed the door, he stalked out the back of the villa into the cool night air. The darkness a balm to his overheated skin, if not to the raging pound in his temples and in areas farther south.

As for his flimsy excuse about checking the perimeter of the property, that was a straight-up lie. The only thing demanding his full attention was the raging erection that refused to give him even a second's peace.

Rounding the barn out back, he sagged against the weathered wood and tilted his head up to the starlit ebony sky. His left hand brushed over the nagging ache at his groin. The contact wrenched a hiss from between his teeth and fangs.

Damn, he was in rare shape.

His eyes slammed shut. In an instant, his brain supplied a wealth of erotic images in rapid succession. Chiara shoveling dark soil in the afternoon sun, her face dewy with sweat. Her perfect, teacup breasts beneath that peachy sweater, the dusky nipples tight and all too apparent beneath the soft weave. He groaned at the recollection of her pink tongue flicking out to lick the drop of wine that had stained her plump lips.

"Fuck."

The curse rattled out of his throat, and before he could stop himself, he unfastened the button of his jeans, then yanked the zipper down to give himself access to his erect cock.

Never had he been driven to this state of weakness. He'd been reared on merciless discipline. Iron-hard resolve. Machine-like control.

His body's need for pleasure was a shame that had been beaten out of him—tortured into submission, first by Dragos and the sadistic Minions who served him, then by Scythe himself, years later, after Mayrene.

But physical need was merely a rope that sought to bind him.

Emotional need—like the feelings Chiara stirred in him—was a shackle he refused to don ever again.

He couldn't bear that kind of enslavement. Not again. Not with this Breedmate who tempted him in ways no other woman had before.

Against his will, Chiara filled his senses as he stroked his shaft. He didn't want to picture her, didn't want to recall the sweet scent of her soaped skin and shampooed hair, or the fresh beauty of her face, her wine-stained lips and long-lashed, chocolate-brown eyes.

Damn it, he didn't want to acknowledge the fever that licked through him with every quickening movement of his hand along his cock. He wanted her hands on him. He wanted to hear her breath racing along with her pulse as he pleasured her. He wanted to feel the soft, wet haven of her body gloved around him as he drove them both to the brink of a splintering release.

He wanted all of her.

His veins throbbed with the urge to possess her. To make her his in every way.

"*No.*" The denial ripped past his teeth and fangs, but it was too late. He came hard into his own hand, images of Chiara filling his mind, his senses, his blood.

He shuddered with the force of his release, and with the depth of his self-disgust. Not only for the pitiful indulgence he'd just succumbed to, but for the stupidity of his motivation.

If he thought his desire for Chiara could be swept from his system so easily, he recognized the fallacy of that idea now.

Because her name still echoed through him with each heavy breath he dragged into his lungs. Her scent still clung to his memory, sweet and enticing. The fierce hunger that had driven him outside like a base animal still hammered through his veins.

There was no taking this edge off.

He glowered back at the villa, watching as the sole

light in the place—Chiara's bedroom—winked out. No chance in hell that he could return inside now to seek his own bed. Not when it was only a few paces away from hers.

How he would endure another night—or worse, a handful more—he didn't want to contemplate.

No, the best thing he could do was keep a healthy distance from his lovely charge until he'd done his job and could get the fuck out of here.

Scythe had never been one to ask for favors, but he sent a silent prayer up to the fathomless night sky, begging for mercy he knew he damned well didn't deserve.

CHAPTER 6

Chiara stood at the back door of the villa and stared out at the torrential late afternoon rain, her frame of mind as dark as the ominous sky.

Three days. Three days cooped up in this house alone with Scythe, who seemed at least twice as miserable about that fact as she was. She'd barely seen him since the second night, after he'd made it crystal clear that he couldn't wait to be finished with his mission.

The villa was a large, sprawling space, but it was practically impossible not to cross paths with someone else in the house at some point.

Unless her forbidding houseguest was deliberately avoiding her.

"Maybe the danger is over," she murmured into her phone, tracing a heart with Pietro's name in it onto the condensation gathered on the window of the door. "Maybe the break-in last week was just a random attack and whoever did it has moved on."

Bella sighed on the other end of the line. "I wish that were the case. Ettore and the other warriors have been doing a lot of digging. The Order seems fairly certain there was nothing random about it."

Chiara frowned at the information. She backed away from the window pane, letting the light-blocking curtain fall back into place. She slumped into a nearby chair with a quiet groan.

"Honestly, Bella, this is getting intolerable. I miss my normal life. I miss my son. Pietro doesn't have to come home if the Order believes it's not safe, but surely the two of us could go somewhere for a while. That way Scythe doesn't have to bother with having me underfoot, and Pietro and I could be together until the Order has done their business."

"I feel for you, but you know we can't risk it. Like Ettore and Scythe said, the best way to stop this individual is to lead him into the Order's hands. Until he's been identified and caught, no matter where you go, this male is a danger to both you and Pietro."

Chiara folded her legs beneath her and let her head tilt back on her tired shoulders. "Well, whatever the Order thinks this male wants with me, I wish it would happen already. I can't stand the waiting."

Or the wanting.

She toyed with the hem of her sweater as she thought back over the past few days. Scythe had been in a dark mood that only seemed to get worse as the days went on. He hardly looked at her anymore, which only made the fact that she couldn't stop looking at him, thinking about him, all the more unbearable.

"What happened to him?" The question blurted out

of her before she could call it back. "When we were at his place in Matera those weeks ago, I heard him tell Pietro that he lost his hand trying to save someone."

And ever since, she'd been curious to know the story. Who had meant so much to the stoic, unreachable former Hunter?

Who had he loved so deeply that he'd risked, and ultimately sacrificed, a piece of himself to try to save?

"You probably know as much about him as I do," Bella replied. "Which isn't saying much, is it? I'm sure I don't need to tell you that Scythe is a hard male to warm up to."

Chiara's mouth twisted. Not being able to warm up to him wasn't the problem at all. She was plenty warm when it came to Scythe. Her skin flushed even now, at the very thought of the hulking, dangerous male.

"If anyone knows anything about Scythe, it'll be Trygg," Bella added. "The rest of us can only wonder what it must've been like to be born and raised as one of Dragos's Hunters. As for what happened to the ones fortunate enough to escape after the Order released them from their enslavement, that's anyone's guess. Can you imagine how hard it must have been for all of those lost boys and men, suddenly set loose to make their way in the world after years or decades spent killing at their Master's command?"

No, Chiara could not imagine. She could hardly bear to consider what Scythe and Trygg and the likely scores of other freed Hunters must have endured—both in and out of Dragos's horrific program.

"Maybe you should ask him."

"W-what?"

"Talk to Scythe," Bella said, as if it were a perfectly

reasonable suggestion. "Ask him yourself about his hand."

Chiara shook her head. "I can't do that."

"Of course, you can. You sit him down and have a real conversation with the male. It would probably do him good to talk to someone. And you, too, *sorella*. What else can the two of you do to occupy your time, sequestered out there by yourselves?"

She nearly choked. A host of indecent possibilities danced through her mind. Thankfully, she was on the phone with Bella, rather than in person. She would be mortified if anyone saw the ruby red flush that now filled her cheeks.

Apparently, Chiara's awkward, prolonged silence was enough to clue Bella in.

"Oh, my God. *Have* you two found something else to occupy your time?"

"No!" Chiara's reply was too quick, too adamant. And possibly too loud. Glancing around anxiously, praying Scythe was nowhere near enough to overhear, she lowered her voice to just above a whisper. "Believe me, you couldn't be more wrong, Bella. At least, not where he's concerned. I'm fairly sure he can't stand me."

Bella scoffed. "Don't be ridiculous. Why on earth would you think something like that?"

"Because he's done little but growl orders at me and stalk around like a caged animal since we left Rome. And I heard him tell Trygg on the phone a few nights ago that he was losing his mind having to—and I quote—lady-sit out here in the middle of nowhere."

"I'm sure you're reading more into it than you should. From what I understand, Scythe has been alone for a good number of years. He's probably not the best company, but I doubt he meant the remark to be anything against you—"

"I touched him."

"Excuse me?"

Chiara pinched the bridge of her nose. "It happened the first night we arrived at the villa. I was trying to tell him that I appreciated him being here, and I don't know what came over me. I... reached out and I touched the scars at his neck. The next thing I knew, I had my fingers in his hair." She blew out a miserable sigh, wanting to melt away in recalled humiliation. "I was practically pawing him, for God's sake."

She waited for her sister-in-law to express her shock or disapproval.

Instead, Bella laughed.

"I'm glad you can find humor in the situation. I was absolutely mortified. I still am. As for Scythe, he was furious. He couldn't get away from me fast enough, and he's been making a point of avoiding me ever since."

"Are you sure?" Bella asked, a smile still lingering in her voice.

"Oh, I'm sure. In the past three days and nights, I've seen him perhaps a total of three minutes."

"No, *sorella*. I mean, are you sure his response to your touch was truly anger? Or was it... something else?"

Chiara went silent, absorbing Bella's words. Against her will, her thoughts raced back to that uninvited moment in her kitchen the first night with Scythe. His expression when she'd caressed his scars had been taut, unfriendly, even seething. Fire had crackled in his obsidian irises, and his fangs had been extended and sharp with warning.

She had dismissed his reaction as displeasure, but

now that Bella made her think on it—really think on it—she wasn't so certain.

And then there was that moment out among the grape vines.

Scythe's kind words, even if delivered with his usual scowl and gruff demeanor. They had shared a few minutes of unguarded conversation. She had confided more in him than she had in anyone for longer than she could recall.

As impatient as he'd seemed to escape the intimacy of their brief talk, she had seen the proof of his reaction on his skin. His *dermaglyphs* had been infused with color in the seconds before he dismissed her to the house.

Those Breed skin markings, which were a more accurate indicator of his mood than anything he could do or say, had been flushed with dark indigo, burgundy and gold. Not black and red and stormy bottle-green.

Not fury, but desire.

"It doesn't matter how Scythe might feel toward me. I'm not looking for anything from him or any other man," she murmured. "I tried that once, and it didn't turn out very well."

"No, it didn't." Bella's tone was gentle with understanding. "I regret that more than you will ever know. You deserved better than my brother, Chiara. And I'm not trying to suggest that I think Scythe might be suitable as a mate to you."

"Then what are you suggesting?" Chiara wasn't sure she wanted to know.

"I've never heard you so much as mention another male's name since you met Sal," Bella pointed out. "Not after he was gone, either. We've been talking for close to an hour today and we keep coming back to Scythe. I just think... I hope that you're not punishing yourself for my brother's failings. I hope you know that it's okay to live your life, Chiara."

"Of course, I know that." But did she, really? How could she claim she'd moved on from Sal's betrayal when she hadn't known another male since? Not that allowing herself to get swept up in whatever was building between her and Scythe would solve any of her problems.

"Maybe Scythe needs the outlet as much as you do," Bella added cheerfully.

Chiara could hardly stifle her outraged gasp. "You are out of your mind! I don't see what possible good that will do either one of us."

As outraged as she was, the indelicate snort that erupted on the other end of the line brought a grudging smile to Chiara's face.

"Oh, *sorella*. If I have to tell you, then my brother was even more of a disappointment than I thought. When was the last time you did something just for yourself? Not for Pietro. Not for the vineyard. Just for you."

Chiara shifted in her seat, suddenly uncomfortable under the weight of Bella's analysis. "I love being Pietro's mother. As for the vineyard, everything I do here *is* for me. I can't think of anything I'd rather do."

"The vineyard is your job, Chiara. Your livelihood. It allows you to stay in the villa and care for your child in comfort. That's not what I mean. I'm talking about you as a woman. A flesh-and-blood woman with needs of your own. When was the last time you let that part of you truly live?"

Was she right? Chiara wracked her brain to think of sometime in the past five, even ten years, when

65

something she'd wanted or something she'd done had been solely about her.

Sal had been her first and only lover. She had been happy with him in the beginning, back when he'd been charming and persuasive, seducing her into a blood bond only weeks after they'd met. She knew he had weaknesses, that he had a selfish streak, but she'd truly believed that her love would change him. She had trusted that their bond would settle him, help him grow into the man she hoped he could be.

And then Pietro had come along, and the rest hadn't mattered. Things she had wanted, things she had desired, no longer mattered much at all once she had a child to look after. It was only a few months later that Sal's betrayal had come to light. Before she knew it, he was dead at Vito Massioni's hand and she and Pietro were alone.

She had been alone ever since.

Three years without a man's companionship.

Three years without a man's touch.

She had closed that part of herself off... or so she'd believed.

She thought of Scythe and instantly shivered. How could someone so imposing, so hard and dangerous, make her feel so warm and soft inside?

How could he make her *want* so intensely?

As if conjured by the will of her subconscious, Scythe took that precise moment to emerge from somewhere in the villa. Silent on his feet, as stealthy as the killer he truly was, he stepped into the room. His jet-colored gaze glanced her way only briefly, but it was enough to set her pulse thrumming in her veins.

She turned her back to him in the chair, her cheeks

still warm from all of Bella's probing observations and outlandish advice.

"Thank you for checking in on me, *sorella*. Like I said, everything is just fine here."

"Ah," Bella replied, her tone sage with understanding. "So, he's there in the room with you now, is he?"

Chiara tried to sound casual. "That's right."

"Wonderful. Let me speak to him."

"Absolutely not!"

Bella's giggle was bright and filled with a happiness that made Chiara's heart clench. "All right, then. Just promise me you'll think about what I said."

Think about it? She doubted she would be able to put a single word of it out of her mind. Especially so long as Scythe was standing in the room with her, sucking out all of the air.

"I have to go now," she told Bella. "I haven't eaten a thing all day and I'm starv—"

The sound of the back door closing hard at Scythe's heels brought Chiara's head around sharply. He was already gone, heading out into the punishing rain. The gathering darkness swallowed him up.

"I'll talk to you again soon," she murmured into the phone, feeling a pang of disappointment light in her breast.

At least she didn't have to worry about Bella persuading her to do something foolish with him.

Scythe seemed determined to keep as much space between them as possible.

CHAPTER 7

A nother flash of lightning lit the dark sky and Scythe grimaced.

Drenched to the bone and miserable with cold, he made one more needless perimeter check of the vineyard property. As much as he preferred to avoid being in the house, he resigned himself to the fact that he couldn't stay outside in the rain all damned night. He'd been a lot of bad things in his life, but coward had never been one of them.

To prove that to himself, he stalked in from the vineyard and up the stoop to the back door of the house. Through the rain-streaked glass, he paused there, watching Chiara cleaning up after her dinner. His stomach rumbled with hunger of his own as his gaze locked on the sight of her from behind.

She wore black leggings and an oversized, cream sweater that hung off one shoulder, seeming to cling there by sheer force of will. His mouth went dry as he imagined hooking one finger under the neckline and sending the whole thing pooling around her waist. Staring transfixed, he watched her walk over to the table and lean over it, wiping down the surface. Her small, lean body stretched out in an elegant line, and her hips rocked gently with each stroke of her hand.

Scythe tightened his fist at his side, refusing to let himself carry the vision of her into a fantasy he couldn't afford to entertain. His jaw set firmly, rigidly, the points of his fangs biting into the flesh of his tongue.

She must have felt the weight of his gaze on her through the window. On a start, she wheeled around, eyes wide with fear. She relaxed only fractionally upon seeing it was him standing there, not the monster who'd attacked her.

Scythe grunted low under his breath.

If she only knew how dangerous he actually was to her safety and well-being. Especially when he was fighting a raging erection and a thirst for the vein that raced so frantically in her neck, he could see it where he stood.

Her free hand came up to her throat, whether a subconscious act of defense or in an effort to calm her fluttering heartbeat, he wasn't sure.

She met him at the door before he could decide if he really wanted to open it.

"You're soaked," she said, frowning as she swung the panel wide. "Come in, Scythe, for God's sake."

He stepped in begrudgingly, feeling like a clod for the way he dripped all over her little welcome mat. She disappeared into the small bathroom down the hall, returning a moment later with a thick, fluffy towel in her hands.

"It's a good thing the Breed can't get sick. You might've caught your death out there in the rain and cold."

He stared at her, telling himself he didn't want or need her concern, despite that it kindled something inside him that felt too pleasurable, too affectionate, for his liking.

"Here," she said, thrusting the towel at him. "Dry off and get warm."

She backed away, but it took a long moment before she finally turned to resume her cleanup of the kitchen. And now here he was again, trapped in this rambling house with her. Strange how the space could be so large, yet he was still distinctly aware of her at all times. He felt her presence in his marrow, even when she wasn't in the room with him.

And when she was? The air sizzled with awareness that he could neither shake nor deny.

She felt it too. He couldn't fool himself by pretending the attraction between them was his burden alone. What would she do if he crossed the floor and took her in his arms? What would do if he sealed his mouth over hers the way he'd been dying to do since that first night they arrived?

If he grazed his fangs over the delicate vein at the side of her neck, would she scream and push him away? Or would she melt against him and let him breach that sacred font and take his fill?

The groan that sounded in the back of his throat seemed to fill the quiet of the kitchen.

Jesus, how long had it been since he fed?

He mentally ticked off the days, shocked to realize it had been almost a week. Only a week since he'd come here with Chiara, yet it felt like an eternity. An endless test of his discipline, not to mention his threadbare honor.

The Order still had incomplete intel and it appeared they were coming to a dead end on Chiara's assailant. His surveillance on the property had turned up nothing more threatening than a random deer or fox. His internal warning system had been quiet, too, which was making him twitchy. Sooner or later, something had to break. He hoped like hell it wouldn't be him.

Fact was, the longer he denied his body nourishment, the more he put Chiara's life at risk. Not only from his own base impulses, but from the threat he knew down to his bones was coming.

"I need to shower," he muttered gruffly to Chiara's back. Christ, did everything he said to her have to sound like an accusation? Awkwardly, he cleared his throat. "Thank you for the towel."

"Of course." She gave him a small nod, her pretty mouth curving in a smile that made his pulse kick. "You're welcome, Scythe."

As much as he wanted to soak for hours under the scalding spray of the shower, time away from his watch was time he left Chiara unguarded and vulnerable. After scrubbing himself with soldier-like efficiency, he toweled off and dressed in a dry black T-shirt and black jeans.

He had hoped to find her retired to her bedroom as she'd done every night before, but instead she was curled up in a cushioned chair in the living area with a glass of wine in her hand and a paperback book spread open in her lap. Her feet were bare, tucked to the side of her on the large chair, her tiny red toenails looking like glossy droplets of blood against her pale skin.

Scythe steeled himself to the guileless temptation of her.

"Everything okay outside tonight?" Her soft, husky voice poured over him like an elixir and he let his eyes drift shut for just a moment before he entered the room.

"We're battened down and secure. No sign of anything out of the norm. The same as it's been out there every other damned night," he added irritably.

She blew out a sigh and placed her book and wineglass on the coffee table. "I feel like we're both prisoners here. Are you going as stir-crazy as I am?"

He grunted in reply, slanting her a dark look that surely conveyed more than any words could. Because he was too keyed-up to sit, he prowled the large living room, glancing with reluctant interest at the tall cases filled with well-worn books, knick-knacks, and framed snapshots of Pietro from infancy to recent times. Chiara's things. The things that cataloged her life here at the villa, things that meant something to her.

Scythe moved on, drawn to the far side of the room, not only because it was farthest from her at the moment, but because his gaze had caught on something else now. Tucked into a quiet corner near an invitingly warm fireplace were a small pedestal table and two chairs. The table was, in fact, a chessboard. Arranged on top of it was a set of carved marble pieces... and one odd object on the board, duller and darker than the others.

Scythe recognized it instantly.

He picked up the carved stone lion. He knew the weight of it in his hand by memory. His fingers knew every curve and flaw in the piece, which he had shaped himself more than a decade ago. Before he'd lost his right hand.

Before he'd lost Mayrene and the little boy he'd originally gifted with the piece.

"The white knight has been missing from this board for years." Chiara stood right next to him, her soft fragrance and quiet voice jolting him to attention. When he swiveled his head to look at her, she offered him a mild shrug. "Pietro thought your lion should take its place."

Scythe felt his mouth twist into something between a scowl and a smirk as he replaced his crude carving on the checkered field with its snowy, richly detailed comrades.

"Do you play?"

He shrugged. "I know the rules of this one, but I've never played. I'm not much for games."

"Why not? Don't you like to have fun?"

Fun? That word wasn't part of his lexicon. "Games are pointless diversions," he replied automatically, his Hunter's upbringing speaking for him. "I don't like to waste time."

"If you enjoy something, then it's never a waste of time." She tilted her head at him. "What's the matter? Have you got something more pressing that you need to be doing right now? Maybe you need to go check the motion sensors in the rain for another few hours?"

Was she mocking him?

Worse, did she suspect his avoidance of her had less to do with his efforts to carry out his mission than it did with his fear of being near her for any length of time?

"Come on, Scythe. We're both at our wits' end out here with nothing to do but watch the clock and wait for something to happen." She gestured to the chessboard. "Let's play. I promise to go easy on you, since it's your first time."

Even if he wanted to refuse, the words died on his tongue. His body tense with awareness and want of her, he stood unmoving as she seated herself on the white side of the board and waited for him to join her.

"One game," he muttered, settling in behind the row of black pieces.

He wondered if she had any clue how she affected him. The grace of her movement, the cameo beauty of her face, even the pop of scarlet on her shapely little toes, made his blood thrum.

Now, backlit by the crackling fire, he realized that beneath the sweater that continuously tormented him by sliding off her shoulder, she wasn't wearing a bra.

His cock surged, leaving him no choice but to shift in an attempt to get more comfortable. Which wasn't going to happen. Not with Chiara seated within arm's reach of him, her perfect breasts naked under the soft weave of her clothing.

She glanced at him, humor dancing in her dark brown eyes. "You're not having second thoughts already, are you?"

Second and third thoughts, in fact, but none of them strong enough to convince him to get up from the table. He chuckled, choosing to ignore the strained sound of it. "Maybe you should be the one to reconsider. I feel it's only fair to warn you that I always play to win."

"Then this should be interesting." She grinned as she moved a pawn into the playing field, opening the space in front of her king. "Because so do I."

He arched a brow. "I thought you said you'd go easy on me."

"That was before you admitted you're not going to

show me any mercy."

She was still smiling as he slid one of his pawns out to block hers. Without hesitation, she moved diagonally and claimed his piece. Scythe cursed under his breath.

Her face gave away nothing as he reached for another pawn—the neighbor to his forfeited one—and moved it two spaces forward on the board.

As soon as his fingers left the piece, her hand hovered over her queen. Scythe groaned, instantly seeing his mistake.

"Ah, fuck."

Chiara's queen slid diagonally across the board, into a space that left his king wide open and unprotected. None of his other pieces could block her next, fatal move. She smiled sweetly. "Checkmate."

"Another round," he growled, determined to redeem himself.

She actually had the nerve to giggle as they set the pieces back in place and began a second, more cautious, game. He avoided falling into her traps, even though he had to admire her strategic intellect and her ability to recover from all of the snares he attempted to lay in front of her. The game was a challenge and a welcome diversion, but after a while, he realized he was simply enjoying her company.

"This set is a masterpiece," he remarked, picking up the white rook he'd captured and turning it over in his hand to watch the firelight glimmer across its surface. The pieces were beautifully carved, the white ones honed from snowy marble, the black ones made of polished onyx. Even the board was a work of art, fashioned out of one solid piece of walnut that gleamed with polish.

He had found carving to be a good outlet for his

restless energy after he and the other Hunters had been freed. He'd done all right with his work, but this skill was far beyond his own.

"Sal's father made this for us after we were mated. It was our first anniversary gift from him." Chiara's mouth curved in a bittersweet smile as she lovingly stroked the surface of the board.

The reminder that she'd once been mated to another male sent a blast of white-hot jealousy coursing through Scythe, but he tamped it down ruthlessly.

She is not yours, Hunter.

"It's a generous gift. It must have taken him all year to create such a work of art."

"My father-in-law was a generous, caring man." A hauntedness filled her eyes in the moment before she glanced away from Scythe. "I wish I could say as much for his son."

"How did you and Sal meet?" Not that it was any of his damned business or concern, but there was a part of him that wanted to know. Another part of him just wanted to keep this moment going, to absorb every detail about this extraordinary woman for as long as he could.

"We met five years ago. I lived and worked in the next town over. On breaks and weekends, I used to ride my bicycle out here to the Genovas' vineyard and sit on the far hill. It was my secret place—or so I thought. One night I fell asleep out among the vines and when I woke up, I was staring at one of the most handsome Breed males I'd ever seen. He was polite and charming, and instead of railing at me to get off his land, he insisted that he see me home."

Scythe grunted. "Sounds like a perfect gentleman."

"He was... at first. I didn't know about the gambling or the lying until after we were mated. Then he couldn't hide who he truly was. I felt every betrayal through our bond." She drew in a breath, then let it out in a long sigh. "I thought he would change—if not for me, then for our baby—but he didn't. I don't think he was capable of changing."

"What about your own family? Did they know anything about this?"

She withdrew now, sinking back against her chair. "Sal was the only family I had. I was orphaned as a baby and left at a Darkhaven shelter. A nice Breed family took me in, but everything fell apart after First Dawn."

Scythe nodded grimly, having witnessed that volatile period in the Breed's history firsthand. After the human population learned they shared their world with blood-drinking predators, chaos erupted. Wars raged for years following that first morning after the news broke. Violent clashes between mankind and the Breed took place on a daily basis all over the world. It took time and an enormous amount of diplomatic negotiations between the two races to finally put the violence to an end. But even now, the worlds of man and Breed often clashed.

Chiara swallowed. "During the worst of the wartime, our Darkhaven was raided in the middle of the day by a small army of humans. My adopted father and young Breed brother were dragged out into the sunlight and staked there, left to die while my mother and I were held at gunpoint inside our home."

"Jesus," Scythe muttered. He had heard plenty of horrific stories, but none that put such a sick feeling in his gut—a fury that boiled inside him—at the understanding of what Chiara and her family had suffered.

"My mother was despondent. She had been made to endure both her own pain and that of my father, her blood-bonded mate." Chiara shook her head. "It was more than she could bear. Not even a year later, she took her own life. And then I was all alone."

Scythe wasn't even sure if he was breathing. All of the air in his lungs seemed clogged and unmoving, as heavy as a stone behind his sternum. "You went through all of that, only to end up with a male like Sal?"

"As much as I grew to hate him after everything he did, I will be forever grateful because he gave me this refuge and the miracle of my son. Whatever else happened in my life, as bad as it was, I guess I had to go through it in order to end up where I am now."

"You really believe that?" When she stared at him in question, her dark brows knit together, he shook his head. "Do you really believe in the concept of fate—that everything happens for a reason?"

"I have to believe it, Scythe. Don't you?"

"No." He let a curse roll past the tight line of his lips. "I think it's a crock of shit. I think we live in a fucked up, hideous world. I think bad things happen for no goddamned reason. I think the only miracle is that any of us manage to make it through the day without killing ourselves or the people who count on us to protect them."

She stared at him with her jaw agape, shock and sorrow in her eyes. When she finally spoke, her voice was unbearably tender. "You're not talking about me anymore, are you?"

He got up from the chess table, wishing he'd never

been fool enough to sit down in the first place. All he wanted was to get the hell out of the room, away from her soft gaze and gentle words. But pride refused to let him retreat.

Lightning flashed outside, followed by a boom of thunder so loud, it shook the walls of the house. None of that was more noticeable than the silence stretching between them.

Chiara walked up to him, her movements slow and cautious, as if she were approaching a beast on the end of a very thin leash. Her gaze dropped to his wrist, to the useless stump that remained there.

"All of the violence that was forced on you in Dragos's sick program," she murmured quietly. "It must've been awful. I can't imagine what you went through, what you had to survive in order to be standing here with me now."

He stared down at her, fury and shame raking him from inside. He bit off a low curse. "I hope you never know any of that."

"But I want to. I'd like to understand, Scythe." She took a steadying breath. "I hope you know that you can tell me anything. I wish you would trust me enough to tell me what happened to you."

"Chiara." Her name was a raw warning. "This isn't a good idea."

"I think it's an excellent idea." She stepped in closer to him. "There's something going on here with us. I know you feel it too. I know you don't want to feel it. I'd like to deny it, too, but I can't."

He clamped his molars together, uncertain he'd be able to find the words to refuse her. Not after the days and nights of wanting her. Not when she was staring up at him with such open emotion, such fierce determination.

"I'd like to know where you went and how you managed to live after you were finally released from your Hunter's collar. I wish you'd tell me how you lost your hand, or why you live all by yourself in that tiny place in Matera as if you're paying a penance for some private sin."

When he turned his head away from her, on the verge of retreating for both their sakes before things got any further out of control, she brought her fingers up to his chin. Her touch steered his gaze back to hers.

She shook her head, her dark eyes flashing in the firelight. "Dammit, Scythe, I want to know if you've ever been in love, or if you think that's all just a crock of shit too."

Any hope he had of avoiding this disaster that had been building between them was smashed in that instant. Before he could stop himself—before his brain could even fire off the alarm that he was wading into dangerous waters—Scythe took her mouth in a blistering, breath-stealing kiss.

She melted against him on a moan, her arms circling around his neck to hold him closer. There was little gentleness in this kiss. Their combined need had been denied too long to even hope to contain it.

That door was blown wide open now, and there would be no closing it ever again.

He slipped his hand under the hem of her loose sweater, searching out the petite mounds of her breasts. He'd never regretted his missing hand more than he did now, when he was finally touching this woman.

He couldn't get enough. Using his other arm, he

dragged her further into his embrace, grinding the aching length of his cock against the softness of her body. It was torture, delicious agony, to feel her curves cushion his hard planes and ridges with the barrier of clothing between them.

Chiara must have shared his frustration. She broke their kiss on a gasp, her big eyes drowsy with desire, her lips swollen and glistening. Her scent intoxicated him, flooding his senses with the fragrance of her heated skin and the blood that rushed so swiftly through her veins. Her desire was the most potent drug of all. It called to everything male in him, both his humanity and the part of him that was otherworldly, pure predator.

He skimmed his hand down her side and into the loose waistband of her pants. When he found the drenched, slick cleft of her sex, he nearly combusted on the spot.

"I need you, Scythe." She smoothed her hands over his chest, then twined her fingers in his hair as he stroked her wetness. "I need this. Oh, God. I need to have you now."

He needed her too.

And right now, neither duty nor discipline owned him.

Only desire.

Only this beautiful woman he could not deny and would never deserve.

He growled his agreement and claimed her mouth on a fevered curse.

CHAPTER 8

Shattered.

That was the only word to describe how she felt as he took her mouth in a searing kiss. His body against hers awoke a need she hadn't known in so long—not ever, like this. His fingers on her sex, his wicked caress both tender and tormenting, drove her toward a pleasure that she could hardly contain.

"Scythe." His name was a plea and a demand, the only word she could manage when his touch had obliterated everything but the longing for more of this.

For more of him.

She didn't have the power to heal any of the pains from his past, no more than he could heal hers. But they could lose themselves in this moment, in this passion.

Wet heat pooled between her thighs and she laced her arms around his broad shoulders, sinking deeper into his kiss, writhing against his carnal touch. This was what they both needed so badly. An escape. A refuge. A few precious minutes where the world outside didn't exist, could not touch them. This might be their only chance and she wasn't going to squander a second of it.

Panting, she pulled back, locking gazes with him as she reached for the hem of his T-shirt. "I need to feel your skin."

She barely recognized her own voice. So harsh and full of need. Consumed by an animal yearning she could not curb, she tore off his shirt and looked at him with pure female lust. She heard the low rumble of his growl, though whether he meant it as approval or warning, she couldn't be sure. Nor did she care, not when she was overcome by the tragic beauty of his bared chest and torso.

"Oh, Scythe."

It wasn't pity that robbed her breath as she ran her hands over his muscles and smooth skin. Not even close. As much as she wished he'd never suffered a minute's anguish in his tortured past, she could not deny her complete astonishment—her adoration—of his powerful body bared to her gaze and her touch.

His strong neck was a tangle of brutal scars, a testament to his Hunter origins, but the rest of him was a work of art. Magnificent Gen One *glyphs* swirled in a kaleidoscope of colors and swirling, intricate patterns from his broad, bulky shoulders, to the tapered cut of his abdomen. His immense arms were wrapped in stunning *glyphs*, too, tracking down his biceps and onto his forearms. The markings spread onto the back of his left hand; on his right, they terminated at the abrupt end of his wrist.

"Beautiful," she murmured, reaching out to trace them. He drew in a shaky breath as she smoothed her fingers over his old wound, then blew out a low, heavy sigh as she continued back to his chest, sliding her hands in awe over his warm, hard muscles. "You're beautiful, Scythe."

His amber-lit, onyx eyes closed briefly at her praise, but the stoicism that seemed to ride him so constantly began to fade away as she continued her exploration of him. His bearded jaw relaxed, and the lines that furrowed the center of his brow eased into a different kind of tension. She ran her fingernails over his flesh, raking past hard, flat nipples and lower, scoring his rippled abs lightly as she went.

"Your hands are so soft," he muttered, his dark eyes ablaze with fire now. Those bright sparks flared even brighter as he stared down at her, his fangs gleaming and sharp as he spoke. "Everything about you is so damned soft, Chiara. I don't know how to be gentle. Fuck... I don't want to hurt you."

"I'm not going to break." She pressed a kiss to the drumming space above his heart. "And right now, gentle isn't what I need. Just you, Scythe. Right now, that's all I want."

A rare smile curved his sinister lips. "Thank God."

His mouth descended on hers. As his tongue swept past her teeth in a claiming thrust, he closed his fingers over her throat, his hold on her gentle, yet possessive. Her heart thundered in response, her pulse beating so hard against his palm.

He groaned and took her deeper into his embrace, into his kiss. His mouth was rough, without finesse. His body hard and powerful, vibrating with unbridled hunger and want.

He uttered her name, a gruff noise, unearthly and

thick. His large hand released her throat and slid lower to cup one of her breasts. His nostrils flared as he tugged the wide neck of her sweater lower, baring her to the waist. His eyes fixed on the birthmark that declared her a Breedmate. On her, the small red teardrop and crescent moon symbol rode just beneath her right breast.

He stared at it for a long moment, brushing the pad of his thumb over the mark. When he glanced back up at her, his fangs seemed even longer, sharper than ever. The sight of them sent an ache pulsing low in her belly, and a wild, reckless urge arrowing through her veins.

One bite of his fangs and she would be his irrevocably.

One slip, and her blood would bind them forever.

Scythe seemed all too conscious of that fact too. His touch moved on, lavishing attention on her breasts. He flicked the sensitive peaks of her nipples, then took one into his mouth, groaning as the erect bud tightened even further against his tongue. "I want you naked now, Chiara."

Together they hurried to remove her clothing, then his. If she thought they would make it to her bedroom, Scythe's impatient snarl and rampant arousal told her otherwise.

He tugged her down onto the soft rug in front of the fireplace, positioning her beneath him. She was shameless with him, opening her thighs as he settled between her legs on his knees. His cock thrust upward, a thick spear that surged past his navel. *Dermaglyphs* tracked along its length, the most erotic thing she had ever seen.

Her mouth watered as she gazed at him, and in her core bloomed an inferno of urgent desire.

She nearly screamed when he bent forward to press his mouth to the center of her body. Her sex went molten, pleasure streaking along her nerve endings with each sensual lick and suckle of his mouth. He didn't stop until the first hard jolts of release shook her.

She splintered apart, writhing under the lashes of his wicked tongue.

She groaned in protest when the heat of his mouth left her. Her disappointment didn't last. Her next breath was a jagged cry as Scythe repositioned and impaled her with one slow, impossibly deep thrust.

Fireworks exploded behind her closed eyelids as he set the perfect pace. He was incredibly big, and she was woefully out of practice, but her body seemed to bloom around him. She'd never felt so invaded. So complete.

Despite that she was still coming down from the crest of one climax, another soon began to build as she and Scythe moved as one. Their gazes locked, breath mingling, they fell into a rhythm that was both raw and sublime.

She couldn't hold back her orgasm. She didn't even try. It shattered her, sending her soaring into a place of glittering orange stars and endless night as she held Scythe's intense stare and surrendered herself to the pleasure only he could give her.

His own control lasted only moments longer than hers.

On a hoarse shout, he erupted inside her.

She clutched him as he rocked and shuddered above her, amazed to think that she had been the one to bring this lethal Hunter to his knees. Because as powerless as she was to resist the need that had ignited between them, so was he. She saw that now. She felt it with each powerful movement of his body, and with each roaring throb of his pulse.

After a long while, he finally slowed. With a kiss to her lips, then her brow, he rolled off her and gathered her against him.

For a man who claimed to have no tenderness in him, the way he held her was as if she were made of glass. As if she were the most precious thing he'd ever touched. Not in all her time with Sal—not even in the best of times—had she ever felt such careful attention. Emotion clogged her throat and misted her eyes as she snuggled into Scythe's chest, sighing with comfort under the shelter of his arm.

She wasn't sure how long they lay there, silent but for the tandem beating of their hearts and the quiet rasp of their breathing. Her hand rested on the muscles of his stunted forearm, her fingers idly tracing the beautiful lines of his *glyphs*. She didn't shy away from the rounded end of his wrist. She let her fingers explore this part of him, too, wanting him to know that she accepted all that he was, and what he'd come through in order to arrive here with her.

She was so steeped in contentment, so blissfully lost in what they'd shared, the sound of his deep voice jolted her.

"I was sixteen when my collar came off. By then, I'd already been removed from Dragos's training lab and assigned a Minion handler. I had already proven myself in a dozen different missions, all of them lethal. Killing was all I knew. And then, suddenly, I woke up on my cot and my UV collar was open. It lay on the mattress next to me, cold and unfastened, and by some miracle, I was alive."

Chiara tilted her head and placed a kiss on his arm. "That was the night twenty years ago when the Order freed all of the Hunters?"

"Yes. Although I didn't know that until a long time later. None of us knew it was the Order that hacked into Dragos's laboratory computers and disabled the electronic locks on our collars. All we knew was that we were free." He grunted, irony in the sound. "For many of the Hunters who broke out of the labs or walked away from their handlers that night, freedom was more than they could handle. We were raised to be machines. Nameless. Merciless. We were trained as weapons, nothing more. We didn't know how to function any other way. A lot of us still don't."

"Your half-brothers," she murmured, recalling that every Hunter shared the genes of the same sire—the last of the Ancients, the otherworlders who fathered the Breed race here on Earth. "How many of you escaped the program?"

He shrugged. "I wouldn't know. Probably dozens. Maybe more. Except for a few I've crossed paths with— or swords—there's no telling how many of my Hunter brethren still survive, or where they might be living."

She shuddered to think it. All of those lost Breed boys and full-grown, deadly males, ill-equipped for any kind of normal life, left to make their way in a world that must have seemed so foreign to them. And then there was Scythe. He wore his suffering for all to see.

"Did you lose your hand before or after you had your freedom?" she asked softly.

"After."

He went silent for a long moment, and she waited, giving him the choice to either trust her or keep his pain—and his past—to himself.

"There was a woman I met in Nevada several years after I was freed. A human woman named Mayrene. She had a narcotics addiction that kept her constantly in search of money, shelter, even food. She was peddling herself on the Las Vegas strip when I saw her. At first, I paid her to be my blood Host." He shrugged. "For a few months, it worked for both of us. Then I found out about the boy."

Chiara's breath caught in her breast. Even though she knew it was a biological impossibility for a Breed male to impregnate an average human female, there was a note of affection in Scythe's voice as he spoke about this child.

"Jacob was young, just three years old, the first time Mayrene brought him with her to one of our meetings."

"The same age as Pietro," Chiara murmured, her heart squeezing. "Was he afraid of you? Did he understand that you and his mother were helping each other?"

Scythe chuckled, but there was sorrow in the sound. And regret. "He wasn't afraid of anything, not even me. Very much like your Pietro."

She lifted her head and shifted so she could look at him. "You loved him."

He nodded. "As much as I knew how, I suppose I loved them both. Before I realized it, we'd become something of a family. I protected Mayrene and her son, kept them fed and sheltered so that she didn't need to sell her body anymore. She saw to my needs... when she was sober enough for me to tolerate her. There were times the heroin was so thick in her blood, I wanted to vomit. As for the rest, well, it wasn't long before I didn't want anything she had to offer me. Eventually, I left."

"Did you ever see her again?"

"Yes, I did." His eyes were fathomless obsidian, his mouth a grim line within the trim black beard that framed it. "A few months later, I heard rumors that a gang of Breed males had run through Vegas sweeping up humans to use for game in an illegal blood club. My first thought was Mayrene. I went by her apartment, and she was gone. Jacob too. One of her junkie friends told me Mayrene hadn't been home for a couple of nights. She said Mayrene and the boy had left in a dark sedan with a couple of mean-looking Breed males."

"Oh, my God." Chiara closed her eyes, not wanting to imagine the kind of danger Mayrene and her child had gotten into. "Tell me she and Jacob weren't taken for one of those sick killing clubs..."

Scythe's expression remained stoic, expressionless. "I tracked them down later that night. The club had been set up in a storage facility on the outskirts of the city. The place was locked down and secure, armed Breed guards at every entrance. I could've killed a sentry, but I didn't want to risk alerting the whole place to my arrival. Instead, I found a ventilation duct that let out on the roof. I climbed inside, then crawled through the bowels of the building, following the sounds of humans weeping and screaming."

"Were they—" Chiara couldn't say the words. "Did you find Jacob and Mayrene there?"

He nodded, a tendon pulsing in his jaw. "They were in a basement holding cell, along with half a dozen other humans. Jacob wasn't the only child among them."

Dread rose up her throat as he went on.

"The ventilation duct terminated above the cell. At

the end of it was large generator fan. Those spinning blades were the only thing standing between me and the only two people who mattered to me in my life. I could stop the blades with the power of my mind, but the mental hold would be weakened by my worry for Mayrene and her son." He went quiet for a long moment, no doubt reliving the nightmare in his mind's eye. "I couldn't risk that. I had to immobilize the blades some other way. I managed to jam one of my guns into the fan. The blades stopped, but the engine started to whine and smoke. I called to Mayrene as I knocked out the duct's wire mesh screen. She rushed over with Jacob and I told her to pass the boy up to me, that I was going to pull them both up into the duct."

Chiara sat up, unable to lie still when her heart was hammering with worry. She was too afraid to ask questions, hanging on every syllable as he spoke.

"We worked fast, but black smoke was as thick as fog by the time I had Jacob safely through the blades and inside the ventilation duct with me. I started to pull Mayrene up next, but one of the other women in the cell started screaming for me to help her instead. She crawled up Mayrene's back like an animal. The extra weight dropped them both. I tried again, and this time I was able to pull Mayrene safely up. There wasn't a second to spare. The fan's engine accelerated, and the blades dislodged my gun. The fan was spinning faster, spewing so much smoke it was impossible to see anything in front of me."

He rubbed his hand over his jaw and expelled a curse under his breath. "I knew we didn't have much time before the whole damned place dissolved into gunfire and chaos. I had to get Jacob and Mayrene out of there.

But when I turned and grabbed the boy into my arms, he said, 'What about the others? We have to save them all.'"

Chiara reached out to him, smoothing her fingers over his handsome, tormented face. He didn't withdraw, but he felt a thousand miles away from her now, his gaze bleak.

"I should've ignored the kid. He had no concept of the danger he was in. He didn't know enough to be afraid. He only knew that I had come to save him and his mother, and he thought I could save them all. He was dead wrong."

"Oh, Scythe... You don't have to tell me anything else."

"Yes, I do. I want you to know." His voice was wooden and clipped, as if the words were spilling out of him without his control. "I couldn't ignore Jacob. I didn't want to see the hurt or confusion in his face. I didn't want him to hate me. So, I told Mayrene how to get out of the building the same way I came in. I told her to take Jacob and wait for me on the roof while I got the others out of the cell."

He blinked and lowered his head, a picture of profound pain. "They took off, and I turned back to the spinning blades of the fan. I tried to stall the engine with my mind, but my focus was fractured. All I could think about—all that mattered—was the two people I'd let out of my sight, out of my protection. I realized I had to use something else to stop the blades this time. I couldn't risk forfeiting another weapon. So I reached in and grabbed one of the blades in my grip."

Chiara sucked in a gasp. "You said they were razor sharp."

He nodded. "My right hand was bleeding like bitch, but the blade stayed immobile. I shouted for the captives to give me the children first, then I'd help the adults. No one obeyed. They were all hysterical. The group of them charged the wall and began climbing over one another to be the first spared. It was chaos. It was a disaster in the making. And then I heard Mayrene's anguished scream echo down through the ducts."

"Oh, no." Chiara fought against the sick feeling that wanted to strangle her. "Oh, Scythe... no."

"All of my attention pivoted in that one instant. I lost my focus. I glanced away from the blades and the people scrambling for me to save them. Someone grabbed hold of my hand. I felt my other hand's grasp slip on the fan blade. By then it was too late. The engine wailed as the rotators began to spin again. My hand was gone before I even realized my mistake."

He said it so calmly, as if the loss of limb meant nothing to him. And then she realized why. A broken sob caught in the back of her throat. "Mayrene and Jacob..."

He shook his head. "They were dead on the roof by the time I reached them. The gang of blood clubbers had torn out their throats. There was no saving either one of them."

Tears rolled down Chiara's cheeks, too fast and hot for her to blink them back. She nestled down against his chest, wrapping her arms around him because as much as she needed to be closer, she felt he did too. "I'm so sorry."

"I don't remember much else about that night. I remember killing. I remember wading through rivers of blood—my own and that of the other males I slaughtered in that place. When I woke up, it was nearly sunrise and I was lying in blood-soaked sand near the edge of the desert outside the strip. Another former Hunter found me. If not for Asher, I'd be dead too. He dragged me out of the desert, then kicked my ass to keep me going in the weeks of recuperation that followed."

"I think I like Asher."

Scythe grunted, the first trace of a smile edging his mouth. "I have no doubt you would. And I'm certain he'd like you, which makes me glad the bastard is halfway around the world from here. Or so I assume."

"You don't know for sure?"

"I haven't seen him in many years."

"What about the rest of your brothers who survived the Hunter program?"

He shrugged. "I'm aware of a few, but aside from connecting with Trygg a couple of years ago, I prefer my solitude. Life is simpler that way."

"So, why did you complicate everything by coming here to help me?"

The question blurted out of her, something she'd been trying to understand from the moment she saw him in Rome and learned that he—of all people—had signed on to be her protector.

"You are a complication to be sure, Chiara Genova." He lifted her chin on the edge of his hand. His black irises swallowed her up, flecks of glowing embers mesmerizing her with their kindling heat. "You are also the most extraordinary woman I've ever met. And I would do anything—sacrifice any part of me, including my last breath—to keep you safe."

She didn't know what to say to that, nor did he give her the chance. His mouth claimed hers, kissing her with a reverence that staggered her. She moaned and arched into him, bringing her arms around his neck as her tongue danced with his.

She felt the precise instant that something was wrong.

His body tensed, his kiss halting abruptly. He set her back from him, his head cocked as he stilled and listened to the silence all around them.

"Scythe?" Dread chased away the heat they shared. "What's wrong?"

He let out a chilling snarl. "We've got company. The son of a bitch is here."

CHAPTER 9

Scythe leaped to his feet, pulling Chiara up with him. "Get dressed. Quick." He shoved her sweater and leggings at her, then bent to grab his pants from the floor and hurried to yank them on. "I need you to find someplace safe to hide, someplace with a solid door and a damned strong lock—"

"There's a panic room," she reminded him as she pulled on her clothing. "It's in the wine cellar at the other end of the house."

"Yes. Go there now." He wasn't about to squander precious time donning his shirt or putting on his boots. His main thought—his only concern—was getting Chiara out of harm's way so he could deal with the danger closing in from outside.

She hesitated, watching as he raced to retrieve a pair of loaded semiautomatic pistols from the large oak bar in the living room, one of several weapons caches he'd stowed around the villa in preparation for any chance that he might be caught off-guard by her assailant's return.

When he pivoted back to her, her face was stricken with dread. "Are you sure it's him? You're sure it's the male who attacked me?"

He knew his gaze was grim as he shoved one of the weapons into the waistband of his jeans. "I'm sure."

It had taken his internal radar too long to penetrate the haze of his lust with Chiara, but now his head was ringing with the portent of danger—all of it centered on her. And while he didn't need the sensor alarms to confirm it, in that next instant, one of the tripwires on the property was triggered. The breach sent a pulse of warning to the phone in his pocket.

"Take this." He put one of the firearms in Chiara's hands. "Get to the panic room and lock yourself inside. If anyone breaks through the door, you empty every goddamned round into the son of a bitch. Understand?"

She swallowed, her big brown eyes searching. "I hate the idea of leaving you, Scythe. This is my fight too—"

"Damn it, Chiara. Get the fuck out of here, now!"

His voice boomed with the intensity of his fear. With the depth of his affection for her, a feeling that seemed too big, too profound, for him to acknowledge when all of his battle instincts were on high alert. This woman meant too much to him, more than Mayrene ever had. More than anyone.

He couldn't stand the thought of Chiara in peril. The thought of her being injured... or worse?

He shook his head, a violent curse erupting from between his teeth and fangs.

He wasn't sure who needed the comfort more, but he couldn't resist drawing her close, however briefly. He kissed her lips, then hugged her tight before setting her away from him again. "Go, sweetheart. Please."

Her nod wobbled, but she took a step past him.

Too late.

Scythe knew it by the sudden banging in his temples. There was no chance to get her to safety, even if she had fled the room without taking the time to dress. Her assailant was already inside.

The Breed male stood in the wide entryway of the living room. He was immense, as all of their kind were. Light brown hair was slicked back off his angular face, his hooked nose and sharp chin giving him the appearance of a sneering bird of prey.

Scythe might have blown the bastard's ugly head off his shoulders if not for the fact that the male had a nasty looking 9mm trained on Chiara.

"Apparently, I've come late to the party." The Breed male's voice was thick with his Italian accent. A dangerous combination of menace and lust blazed from within his narrowed eyes. "From what I see—and smell—the little bitch who fought me off like a screaming banshee last week is just a common whore. One who'll spread her legs for virtually anyone. How disappointing."

Scythe's urge to fill the vampire's skull with lead was nearly overwhelming. But this asshole didn't matter. He was the walking dead; he just didn't realize it yet.

All that mattered was making certain Chiara stayed out of the other male's reach.

Scythe kept his own weapon and his gaze rooted on the intruder. With his free arm, he subtly motioned for her to come to him. She edged over, and he smoothly swept her behind him, using his own body to shield her.

He was prepared to use his last breath and heartbeat, if it meant the difference between her life and his.

A sneer thinned the other male's lips as his gaze lit on Scythe's maimed arm. "She screeched and struggled with me, yet she let a gimp like you fuck her?" He scoffed. "Was it out of pity, or just poor taste?"

Scythe muzzled the growl that gathered at the back of his throat. He wasn't going to rise to the bait. Killing this pathetic excuse for a male would be a pleasure, but he hadn't forgotten his promise to help the Order collect vital intel. His first, most important priority was the one huddled at his back, but duty bound him to do whatever he could to assist his brother and the other warriors.

He glowered at the hulking male, both of them caught at an impasse between the business ends of their weapons. "What kind of sick bastard makes a habit of terrorizing defenseless mothers and children?"

The sneer turned even darker. "One who means to have vengeance."

"Vengeance." Scythe hissed the word. "What the fuck does this woman have to do with that?"

"She owes me. She owes me for what I lost because of her. A new life for the one she took. Whether that's her life or the sons I mean to plant in her as soon as I shackle her to me by blood, I don't really give a damn. But I will collect."

"He's insane," Chiara gasped. "I never saw him before he broke in here last week. I have no idea what he's talking about."

"You should step aside," the male warned, fire flashing in his eyes. "I don't intend to leave here without her this time."

Scythe met the sparking animosity with fury of his

own. "You'll have to come through me first."

"Oh, I don't think so."

Scythe's senses stirred abruptly, jabbing through the veil of his concern for Chiara. He had been unable to recognize the threat of her assailant in time enough for her to get away, but this was even worse.

"Scythe!" Her scream pierced him to his marrow. The air went acrid with the scent of another Breed male, poised to attack and moving in on them from behind.

Scythe swiveled his head, turning his body to meet this new threat, even though he knew the inattention to the enemy in front of him was liable to cost him dearly.

And it did.

The second male fired his gun. The shot rang out and Chiara's pained cry felt like a bullet ripping through him instead of her. She went down. The scent of her spilling blood staggered him. It shredded him.

He roared, pulling the trigger on his semiauto and bellowing as the rounds made hamburger of the shooter's face and skull.

He heard other gunfire around him, smelled the pungent odor of smoke and heated metal—and blood. His own and Chiara's. But in those frantic seconds, all he saw was rage. Red, blinding rage.

When he pivoted to deliver the same lethal fury on the first male, he found nothing but empty space. The son of a bitch had fled.

Chiara moaned.

He dropped down beside her, relief washing over him to see that she was alive.

"Scythe." Her beautiful brown eyes flipped open, searching for him.

"I'm here, love."

"The other male—"

"Don't worry about him. He's gone now, but I'll find him. I won't rest until I do."

He smoothed her hair from her face, cursing when he saw the smear of blood he left on her brow. He'd been hit, too, evidently. Not that he gave a damn about that.

Chiara was injured. Safe for now, but bleeding from a gunshot wound in her shoulder. Fury coiled in his gut. He would eviscerate the male who got away. If he had his choice, he would make the pain last a lifetime.

She winced and reached over to her wounded shoulder. The sleeve and front of her sweater were scarlet with spilled blood—a good deal of it his.

"Lie still," he said, but she ignored his order, already pushing herself to a sitting position.

"I'm okay." She frowned as she covered her wound with her hand and looked up at him. "It hurts, but I'll be—" Her face paled. "Oh, my God. Scythe, you've been shot too."

He shrugged, wholly unconcerned with his own injuries. That is, until he glanced down and realized the extent of them.

Bullet holes pierced his bare chest and torso in several places. Those were problematic enough. But it was the gunshot wound that had ripped into the biceps of his left arm—his only fighting arm—that made a cold worry settle in the pit of his stomach.

"I'll live," he assured her. That much he was certain of.

But given that he hadn't fed in a full week?

His healing would take time he didn't have. Dawn would be breaking in a few hours, but he had no idea how he was going to manage to protect Chiara once night fell again and the Breed male bent on his private vengeance came back to take what he thought he was due.

Because Scythe had seen the determination—and the madness—in the vampire's eyes. He was gone for tonight, but not gone for good. He would return for Chiara, and when he did, Scythe knew the son of a bitch would not be coming alone.

CHAPTER 10

Chiara sucked in a hiss of pain as she reached into the cupboard for a coffee cup that next morning. The bullet graze could have been much worse, but it still hurt like hell. Her shoulder felt as if it had been used as a punching bag, then lit on fire just for good measure.

But as uncomfortable as she was, she knew it was nothing compared to how Scythe must be feeling.

The sight of him last night, bullet-riddled, bleeding—all because of her—was something she would never forget. She could never repay him for how he'd protected her from the madman who was holding her responsible for a crime she couldn't understand.

Scythe had been willing to give his life for her last night; she had no doubt.

God, he almost had.

He was Breed, so his advanced physiology meant he could heal from all but the most catastrophic injuries. Gunshot wounds to the body were rarely fatal, but it would take time and blood to heal them.

Scythe had neither.

He had dismissed her concern last night, insisting on cleaning up the mess from the confrontation and then disposing of the body outside so the rising sun could ash the remains. He had refused her help in dressing his wounds, assuring her that he'd dug plenty of bullets out of his body before. He argued that he had patched himself up hundreds of times in the past and that last night was no different.

Except it was.

She knew it, even if he refused to admit it.

Scythe hadn't fed since the night they left Rome a week ago. For a Gen One, even without the gunshot wounds to contend with, he was treading dangerously close to the edge of depletion.

She heard his deep voice in the other room, so she poured a cup of coffee and padded out of the kitchen in her sleep shirt and pajama bottoms to find him. His phone pressed to his ear, he prowled the living area like a cat in a cage. He was showered and dressed in jeans and a black T-shirt, a fresh bandage on his left arm. From across the room, she could see a small red rose of blood already seeping through the clean white wrapping.

He glanced her way as she stepped into the room. His brows were furrowed, his mouth bracketed with deep lines. A lot of the color was faded from his face, making him look stark and sallow, even though he was still formidable and easily the most brutally handsome male she'd ever seen.

Once his onyx eyes fixed on her, they stayed rooted there, inky dark and grave. Impossible to read. "I'll call again when things are in motion on this end, Trygg.

Expect to hear from me within the hour."

"You called the Order," she said as he ended the call.

"Yes." He slid the phone into his pocket, his voice edged with an odd resignation. "They needed to be apprised of the situation."

She nodded. She couldn't deny feeling a vague sense of relief to hear that he wasn't going to let pride or any other foolish idea keep him from enlisting the warriors' help. "Will we be returning to Rome, or will the Order be coming here?"

"Neither." The answer made her heart lurch. "The warriors have a Rogue problem in Florence that's grounded them all in that city until nightfall tonight. But I didn't ask them to come here. This fight is mine now. As for you, you'll be going back to the Order's command center without delay. The daylight will be your best protection until you reach Rome."

"What?" *No.* Everything inside her rejected the idea. She didn't like this plan at all. She didn't like the grim finality of his tone. "What about you?"

"I'm going to finish what I came here to do."

She set her cup down on the nearby bookcase, bristling and defiant. But she was terrified too. Not so much for herself, but for him. "You're in no shape to do anything. Scythe, you were shot multiple times last night. Your left arm took the worst of it. I realize you're a big, strong Hunter who's probably seen more combat and violence than ten other Breed males put together, but this is crazy. My God, this is probably suicidal."

He grunted in dismissal of her concern, turning away to inspect the arsenal of firearms and blades that he'd assembled on the surface of the bar.

"You won't be ready," she argued. "Your wounds

won't heal that fast and you know it. You need rest and you need to feed—"

"Trygg is arranging to send a blood Host from a neighboring town to service me."

Chiara staggered, absorbing the news as if she'd been punched in the stomach. Feeding from a human was as routine for him as her morning coffee was for her, but this felt different. This felt like a goodbye.

This felt like rejection of everything they shared.

She had no claim on Scythe; she knew that. But after they'd made love last night, after they'd let each other into their pasts, into each other's hearts, a part of her belonged to him. A part of her had belonged to him even back in Matera—this lethal assassin with the haunted eyes and the core of honor he didn't understand that he possessed. A part of her had loved him from the moment he'd given Pietro that carved stone lion.

So now, as badly as he needed nourishment, the thought of him feeding from someone else—male or female—tore something loose inside her.

Whether he understood how viscerally it affected her or if he felt the same way, too, she couldn't be sure. But Scythe's expression hardened, his gaze finally breaking contact with hers.

"I don't want you to be here when the Host arrives," he murmured, staring at the floor. "Now that it's morning, it will be best if you leave the villa as soon as possible."

"No." At her sharp reply, his head snapped up. She ignored his furious scowl, glaring right back at him. "No, I won't. This is my home. I'm not going anywhere."

"Chiara, I don't need you here—"

"Yes, you do." She stepped forward, not stopping

until she was standing right in front of him. "You *do* need me here, Scythe. And I'm not going to run away while you try to gain your strength so you can fight a battle that belongs to me. Not after what we shared last night."

As much as she loathed the thought of him putting his life on the line for her, it terrified her to think that he would do so at anything other than his physical best. Human blood would ease the pain of his hunger and nourish his body, but it wouldn't heal his wounds. Not fast enough for him to fight.

Anger flared in the dark pools of his eyes. "I'm not asking for your agreement on this."

"No," she replied. "And I'm not asking for yours. I'm not leaving you. I won't let you take a human's vein when I know that a Breedmate's blood—*my blood*—is the only thing that will truly heal you."

He reared back on his heels, uttering a tight curse. But even as he did, she could see the bright white tips of his fangs already stretching from his gums.

She saw the torment and the want—the thirst—in his anguished face.

As much as he needed the gift she was offering, they both understood what drinking from each other would mean. One taste of her blood on his tongue would bind him to her for as long as they both lived. There would be no other woman for him, Breedmate or human. He would crave only her. And if she drank from him, the same would be true for her. They would be bound eternally. Unbreakably.

"You need to go, Chiara. Damn it, you need to go right now."

The words were like gravel, jagged and rough, but the look in his eyes... it was pure, desperate desire. There was no hiding his fangs now. They gleamed razor-sharp, filling his mouth.

A grimace twisted his handsome, tormented face. Growling something low under his breath, he turned away from her and went back to preparing his weapons for the battle that would be coming all too soon.

"I won't go," she said, resolve taking root inside her. "I won't leave you. I'm not going to walk away when I'm the only one who can truly help you right now."

She picked up one of the blades on the table. There was no question as to what she intended to do. Not a shred of doubt or apprehension in her mind.

She sliced the dagger across the soft flesh of her wrist.

Scythe's hiss was even more pained than hers. He wheeled around as the first scarlet drops swelled from her open vein. His eyes seared her, ablaze with amber light, his face contorted with shock and anguish.

"Damn you, woman." His low voice didn't sound like anything from this earth. It was as dark as she'd ever heard it. So deadly it sent a shiver through her bones, into her veins. If she had forgotten how lethal this Gen One Hunter was, his face and voice were stark reminders now.

She had enraged him, possibly even earned his hatred with this impulsive act. But she didn't tremble. She didn't shrink away, not even when he stalked toward her, radiating a fury she'd never felt or seen in him before.

She held her bleeding arm out to him, her eyes fixed on his. "Take it, Scythe."

"You don't know what you're saying." His scowl deepened along with the otherworldly edge of his voice.

"You'll be trading one unworthy mate for another. I'm no better than Sal."

"Yes, you are." She shook her head, tears stinging the backs of her eyes. "You are worth ten of him. You're so much more than that, Scythe. You are the kindest, most honorable man I've ever met. I'll never know a man as noble or courageous as you. I'll never want anyone more."

He made a sound somewhere between anguish and denial. "Chiara—"

She silenced his mounting protest with a kiss, then drew back from him, extending her arm between them. Blood splashed onto the floor, pulsing from her opened vein. "It's yours, Scythe. Just as I am... if you want me."

His large hand closed around her wrist, his nostrils flaring as he held her in his grasp. He shook his head, his eyes hot with need and hunger and something deeper.

"My brave, beautiful Chiara," he muttered. "God help you if you want me as much as I want you."

He brought her wrist to his mouth. Then he sealed his lips over her opened vein and began to drink.

CHAPTER 11

S cythe let out a helpless groan as the first taste of her coursed over his tongue.

For all his tough talk and self-castigation, this female was the one thing that truly made him weak. She wrecked all of his defenses, tore down all of his walls. Her beautiful heart and fierce courage left him vanquished, just as surely as her blood was making him strong, healing the damage of his flesh and bones.

In truth, she was healing him in ways far more profound than that.

She was his. Even before he'd taken her vein to his mouth. In his heart, she had been his all along. And now it was real. Now, it was forged in blood.

Breakable only by death—his own, or hers.

He'd never had better reason to keep breathing than he did now.

And he would not fail her.

He couldn't live with himself if he did.

She moaned as he suckled her wrist, his throat working greedily, drawing her in vitality, her life. Her love.

As incredible as it felt to know that her cells were feeding his, it was the taste of her affection toward him—the stunning depth of her emotions—that was the most powerful revelation.

She loved him.

He felt it through the new bond that was taking root between them. His emotional and psychic link to her gained more strength with each heartbeat. Her blood was alive in him, infusing his body with energy so intense he could feel it streaking through him like lightning. It was her energy. Her essence. It throbbed deep into his marrow and into his senses, a strange, vibrant hum that grew stronger with each sip he took from her.

He had never experienced anything so awe-inspiring, so humbling.

"Chiara," he murmured, sweeping his tongue over her wound to seal it closed. He looked up at her and found her watching him with infinite tenderness. With so much soft regard, it staggered him. "My angel."

She swallowed, nodding shakily. "I'm yours," she whispered, reaching out to caress the side of his face. "And you're mine."

"Yes." He was too far gone to pretend otherwise.

He'd been an idiot to think he could push her away right now, even if it was the safest, kindest thing he could do for her. She was his—not because of the blood bond he'd so selfishly taken, but because she was the only woman he'd ever truly wanted.

The Breedmate he'd never dreamed he could deserve.

He wouldn't deserve her—not until her safety and Pietro's was secured.

But he wanted her. Christ, how he wanted her.

"Come here, love." His fangs crowded his mouth, but he took great care to kiss her gently, determined to show her that he did have some capacity for control, even if it was threadbare when it came to her.

He gathered her against him, and soon the warmth of her body, the softness of her curves, incinerated all of his good intentions. Need resonated through his whole body, heating his blood, settling in his bones. If he thought his craving for her had been torture before, he knew better now.

Spearing his hand into her hair, he wrapped the silky mass around his fist, once, twice, and then tugged her head back to take his kiss deeper.

Somewhere distant, in the back of his mind, a warning bell jangled, urging him to slow down, to leash the overwhelming spike of his hunger for her. But he was drowning in Chiara... the taste of her, the scent of her skin, and soon, that warning bell was nothing more than a memory.

He plunged his tongue into her mouth to tangle with hers as she whimpered and squirmed against him. For one terrifying second, he thought she was trying to escape him, but then her arms slid around his waist and pulled him closer still. She was so petite, her breasts pressed against his stomach, her legs twining with his.

He drew back, desperate for more.

"I need to be inside you," he muttered, his voice no more than a growl as he slid his hand free of her silky locks and skimmed it down her neck, pausing to trace her delicate collarbone.

She shivered, goose bumps breaking out on her skin as he drew her shirt over her head and bared her lovely body to his gaze. No panties beneath her pajama bottoms, which she shimmied out of as he watched, fevered and vibrating with arousal.

He'd never been a man inclined toward poetry. Hell, he'd never been inclined to wax rhapsodically on anything, but Chiara made him wish he had the words to express just how beautiful she was to him. Speech failed him as he stared down into her face now.

He had no words, but inside, every fiber of his being sang with emotion.

"Mine," he said simply, possessively. Reverently.

He didn't feel the pain of his injuries or the limitation of his missing hand as he lifted her into his arms. He carried her into her bedroom and placed her beneath him on the mattress. She helped him shed his clothing, her fingers as light as butterflies as they skimmed over his bandages.

Her brow knit with concern. "Are you sure, Scythe? Your injuries—"

"My injuries are nothing. Your blood is already mending me." It was true. He could feel his bullet-torn muscles and bones healing just moments after he took the first sip of her blood. He smiled down at her, blatantly carnal. "As for the rest of me?"

He laced his fingers with hers and dragged her hand lower to cup his heavy erection. Her gasp tangled with his low hiss as she closed her fingers around his cock. He was harder than he'd ever been before, and so large his girth exceeded her petite grasp.

He thrust into her firm, silken hold. "Your blood has made all of me stronger."

"Let me feel it, Scythe. I need you inside me now." Her plea was breathless, but filled with demand. She shifted beneath him, wrapping her leg around the back of his thighs and arching her hips in sultry invitation.

Scythe couldn't have denied her if he were bound and chained under the full blaze of a noonday sun. He had to have her. His need swamped him, pushed everything else to the furthest corners of his mind.

He and Chiara would be safe until night fell again. For now, there was just the two of them. Just this hunger for each other that owned them both.

With his weight braced on his right arm, he slid his hand under her and tilted her hips to meet his invading thrust. He sank in deep, swallowing her cry in a kiss that matched the ferocity of his passion. He plunged hard and wild, unable to take it slowly when every primal instinct within him was pounding with the urge to claim her.

As his woman.

As his mate.

As the future he never knew he wanted until her.

"You're so hard," she murmured, her rich voice husky with wonder and unabashed feminine desire. Her sensuality laid him low and he swallowed a snarl. She moved, taking him deeper, until stars began to burst behind his closed eyelids. "Oh, God... you feel so good inside me, Scythe."

He agreed, although *good* was too paltry a word for what he felt when he was inside Chiara's heat. She fit him as though she were made for him, as if there were no delineation between the point where he ended and she began.

He was bound to her, but these chains were a shackle

he had no desire to escape.

It only made him want more of her.

He wanted her bound to him too.

On a growl, he threw his head back and tried to think of anything but that. Anything but how good her skin smelled and how sweet her blood still tasted on his tongue. How right it would be to seal his mouth to her neck and feel her delectable blood pulse into his mouth in hot, glorious bursts.

As for that other temptation, it refused to let him go. The dangerous whisper of his Breed genetics urged him to complete the circle of their bond by sinking his fangs into his own flesh and feeding Chiara from his opened vein.

He squeezed his eyes shut, clamping down on that part of him that wanted to pretend he was anything close to the kind of mate Chiara deserved.

He wanted to be the man she seemed to believe he was.

Right now, he only wanted to give her pleasure enough to forget what awaited them once night fell again. He focused on her body's responses, pushing her closer to the edge and reveling in her moans and sighs and shuddering gasps.

"Oh, God, Scythe... It's so good. Tell me you feel this too."

"I feel everything," he rasped, astonishment pouring over him.

His own sensation was doubled by the link he had to her now through her blood. Her passion was his. Her mounting climax was a current of electricity that amplified his own building release. She angled to meet his savage thrusts, her plush walls rippling along his length as the first tremors of orgasm vibrated against him. He couldn't stop the rush of heat that rocketed through him. Chiara's orgasm broke at the same time, her cry entwined with his harsh shout.

He'd never felt anything so powerful, so miraculous, as his woman's pleasure spiraling through his senses while his own body quaked with the aftershocks of the most staggering release of his life.

On a low groan, he finally rolled away from her, propping himself against the headboard. Chiara carefully moved onto his lap, her breath still coming in rapid pants as she tenderly ran her fingers over the skewed bandages on his chest. He draped his arms over her, idly stroking her as they both came back down to earth.

She lifted her head, placing a soft kiss to his abdomen. "Are you feeling all right?"

"Isn't it obvious?" He chuckled, shifting his hips so she could feel the already hardening shaft of his erection.

Her brown eyes smoldered with her sexy smile. "I was talking about your injuries. Do they feel any better?"

"After what we just did, I don't feel them at all." He grinned. "But if you're wondering if they're healing, that's an improvement too."

"May I look?"

He nodded, more than willing to have her hands on him. She gingerly peeled away one of the bandages. It came away stained with blood, but the hole in his body was already mending. "Your blood did that, Chiara."

She nodded, glancing back at him with regret in her eyes.

No, not just regret. Fear too.

He felt it streak through her like a chill in the air. He studied her quiet contemplation, dreading the words she seemed to struggle to say.

"You're afraid of this means?" he asked her. "If you're worried that I'll expect anything after all of this is over—"

"What?" Her face collapsed into a confused frown. "No. Scythe, I'm not worried about that at all. How could you think that?"

"But you are worried about something. I can feel your fear, Chiara." He swallowed past the cold knot that was settling behind his sternum. "You regret something. Are you sorry for giving me your bond?"

"Never." Her answer was full of conviction, her brows furrowed as she shook her head in firm denial. "I'll never regret that. Not as long as I live, Scythe."

He reached out to caress her silky cheek. "Then tell me."

"What I regret is that it took this long for us to meet." She released a quiet sigh. "I regret that it was Sal who had me first, not you. And I'm always going to regret that I gave my son such a terrible example of a father."

Moved by her honesty, Scythe collected her against him and placed a kiss to the top of her head. "If we'd met any sooner, you wouldn't have liked me. That much I can promise you. Do I wish you'd been spared the pain Sal caused you? More than you know. As for Pietro, he's got the best mother a child could hope for. None of Sal's failings as a mate or a father can ever diminish that."

She embraced him tighter, resting her cheek against his chest. But that acrid streak of fear still clung to her. On a low curse, he gently drew her up, forcing her to meet his searching gaze.

"Tell me the rest, love. What has you so afraid?"

"I can't stop thinking about what he said—the monster who broke in here last night. I don't know what I ever did to him to earn his hatred."

"With a madman, there's no telling what drives them."

"He said it was vengeance, Scythe. He said he's going to make me pay, either with my own life or..." She swallowed, a shudder coursing over her. "I won't let him take me alive. Not when living means being forced into a blood bond with a deranged lunatic who plans to rape me and make me bear his sons. I'd never survive that kind of hell."

Christ, neither would he. Just the thought of her suffering something so heinous turned his veins to ice. Now that her blood was inside him, Scythe would always have a one-way link to her as long as either of them lived. But that wouldn't prevent another male from activating his own blood connection to Chiara.

Only she could complete the circle. She could not be bound to any male if she had already shared a bond with another.

Scythe's gums tingled with the sudden prickling of his fangs.

He meant what he said—that he would not permit her to fall into enemy hands. He would guard her safety with his life, and he was damned hard to kill. If she were taken, he would hack his way to hell and back to save her.

But if they were separated, the only certain way to protect her in that unimaginable interim was to shield her with his blood.

With his bond.

He lifted her face, needing her to see his eyes and the

determination that lit them. The vow he was about to give her. "He's not going to touch you, love. Not so long as I'm breathing. I won't let it happen." He stroked her cheek. "He won't have your blood or your bond. You can entrust both to me now... if you'll have me."

Her lips parted on an indrawn breath. He felt the spike of her heartbeat, the hope that was now eclipsing her fear. "Scythe, are you saying—"

"You've given me your strength and protection, Chiara. By some miracle of fate, you've given me your love. Now, let me give you mine."

Her quiet sob and the sudden well of joyful tears that filled her eyes was all the answer he needed.

He brought his wrist to his mouth and sank his fangs into the vein that throbbed there. Then he guided her lips to the wound and held her close as she drank.

CHAPTER 12

Night was arriving much too quickly.

Scythe could have lain with Chiara in his arms all day, but there had been important work to do in preparation for the battle ahead. He had secured all portals inside the villa hours ago, but as the afternoon waned toward sunset, he couldn't keep from making another tactical inspection of the house that would need to serve as his bunker.

And there was still one more critical area of his defense that needed to be addressed as well.

Chiara.

Even before they shared their blood, his mind had been made up as to the best means of keeping her out of her assailant's reach. Now that he and Chiara were mated, his resolve had only gotten firmer.

She wasn't going to like his decision, but he would fight that battle when it came too.

As he checked and rechecked the assault rifle he'd

stowed outside the panic room of the villa's wine cellar, his veins began to tingle with the awareness of her approach behind him.

"The sun is going down now," she murmured soberly. "How long do you think we'll have before...?"

As her voice trailed off, he set the Kalashnikov and extra 30-round magazines back into their hiding spots on one of the floor-to-ceiling wine racks, then turned to face her.

"Not long, sweetheart."

"The Order's not going to make it in time to help us, are they?"

"I doubt it." He wasn't going to lie to her. She deserved his honesty, especially when they were about to face this incoming threat together.

A few hours ago, Scythe had phoned Trygg to call off the blood Host and to inform his brother that he and Chiara had mated. The newsflash hadn't earned him any congratulations from Trygg or the Rome commander, Lazaro Archer. And although Scythe had never been one to ask for favors or backup, he had requested both from the Order.

They weren't able to make any promises. There had been a Rogue outbreak in Florence last night. The emergency mission had demanded the work of the entire team from Rome, and the warriors were grounded in that northern city until nightfall.

"Even if they start heading our way now," Scythe told her, "they're still hours away from Potenza."

"I see." She nodded in grave understanding, but he could feel the subtle spike of his brave mate's apprehension. The deep hum that had become a welcome presence since he'd taken his first sip of her blood intensified as a shudder swept over her.

Scythe frowned as he drew her into his arms. "I wish I had sent you away like I wanted to. Keeping you here with me—taking your blood—was the most selfish thing I've ever done."

She shook her head. "No more selfish than me offering it to you. Or me wanting to stay wherever you are. I love you, Scythe."

He could feel her conviction through their bond, but hearing her say the words leveled him. It humbled him. "You honor me too much. But I love you too. More than you can ever know."

A beautiful smile spread over her face. "I do know. I feel it. I feel it like a growing vibration in my bones. I feel it thrumming all the way into my marrow."

Was that what it was? Merely the manifestation of their bond?

He was certain she was the source of the strange undercurrent of power he felt since they had mated, but he didn't get a chance to say the words.

Like a switch being flipped, his internal alarm lit up with warning. Danger was closing in on the vineyard property. They likely had only minutes before the worst of it would be upon them.

He couldn't hide his visceral reaction from Chiara now. His blood told her everything.

He braced himself to feel her terror arc through him, but the sensation didn't come. The strongest emotion he felt from her was resolve. Courage he could hardly reconcile.

"I'm ready," she said, her voice a fierce little snarl as she stepped out of his embrace. She had never been more beautiful than in that moment, her dark eyes glittering with determination. "Let's do this."

"Not *us*, Chiara. Me." He gestured to the open door of the panic room.

Confusion and outrage spiked her blood. She took a breath as if she meant to argue and he shook his head harshly.

"I need you to stay here. Do it for me, so I know where to find you once this is over. When I go out there now, I need to know you're safe."

"And I need to be with you! Dammit, Scythe, we stay together."

"We are together," he said, taking her fisted hand and opening it over the center of his chest, where his heart hammered in time with hers. "You'll feel me with you every second. And I'll feel you."

She swallowed, some of her resistance leaching away. "I don't want anything to happen to you."

"Then help me do my job. Let me focus on killing this bastard so I can come back for you."

A broken cry wrenched from her throat, but she nodded. He guided her into the panic room, his hand on the heavy vault door. As soon as she was inside, she turned and threw her arms around him, kissing him as if she feared it might be the last time.

"I hate this," she whispered against his mouth. "Don't you dare die on me, Hunter."

"I won't," he promised. "Not when everything I've got to live for is waiting for me right here."

Stepping out of her embrace was the hardest thing he'd ever done.

Her eyes stayed locked on his as he pushed the concealed panel closed, sealing her inside.

And not a moment too soon.

His internal warning system was lit up like a fucking Christmas tree. The *tap, tap, tapping* inside his skull became a deafening drum. Inside the pocket of his black combat vest, his phone was buzzing with the triggered alarms of virtually every tripwire on the property.

He slung a crossbow onto his back and slipped two knives into the belt at his waist. A pair of semiautomatic pistols loaded with hollow points bristled in their holsters at his hips. Armed to the fangs and hungry for the fight, he sped out of the wine cellar, then up to the cupola window of the villa, which afforded the best vantage point of the outlying grounds.

Under the blue glow of twilight, half a dozen Breed males prowled in from multiple directions. He wasn't surprised to see that Chiara's assailant had returned with reinforcements. But he hadn't been expecting this.

These feral looking beasts were Rogues, every one of them.

As they stole toward the house, another group emerged from the shadows of the vineyard to encroach on the villa.

Son of a bitch. Scythe's vision bled amber in the second it took for him to assess the incoming threat. His fangs ripped from his gums, battle rage seething into his bloodstream when he imagined what this small army of blood-addicted animals would do if any one of them got their hands on Chiara.

And then there was the male at the center of it all.

Scythe looked for him among the beasts who swarmed the property, but didn't see him. The prickling of his senses told him the bastard was out there somewhere. He would get the bastard. He would end him painfully and permanently. Even if he had to rip through a dozen feral Rogues to do it.

Silently, he lifted the cupola window and climbed out onto the roof. A pair of roosting doves exploded into the sky, flapping their wings in an effort to escape the apex predator in their midst.

Below him on the ground, the pack of Rogues swept in from the vineyard and the lawn, preparing to surround the house. One of them had already reached the back porch.

Scythe dropped down behind the male, as silent as a cat. Before the other vampire even realized he had a problem, Scythe slashed a titanium dagger across the Rogue's throat. The shriek that rang out was short-lived, like its owner, but explosive.

The animal cry rent the night, and suddenly the ground began to rumble with the sound of Rogues charging in from all directions.

CHAPTER 13

A jolt of pain lanced her so brutally, Chiara looked down at her midsection, expecting to find her stomach sliced wide open. Her heart pounded frantically, sweat drenching the back of her neck. She felt another strike bite into her biceps, then a bruising blow to the center of her spine.

But it wasn't her pain.

Not her injuries... *His*.

She rested her forehead against the wall of the panic room, her hand over her mouth to stifle her choked cry. "Scythe!"

It had been unbearable enough to stay behind knowing he was walking headlong into danger, maybe even death. Her only comfort had been the fact that he wasn't afraid. He was confident, determined. Hellbent on coming back to her.

But this?

Feeling his pain the midst of that battle was an

anguish she couldn't endure. Not knowing what he was up against out there was the worst kind of torture. Not being with him when the only thing holding her back was his worry for her safety was an agreement she couldn't keep.

She wasn't trapped in the panic room; she could free herself anytime using the combination lock on the inside.

She had barely let the thought take root in her mind before she was slipping out to the wine cellar on the other side. The sounds of combat and violence outside the villa flew at her like wraiths now that she was out of the sealed chamber.

Dear God, it sounded like war.

One that had the man she loved—her mate—caught in the center of it.

Every fiber of her being railed against that knowledge. Hiding was worse agony than risking her life. She had spent a lifetime cowering in fear and intimidation. No more. The meek, powerless woman she had been before and after Sal no longer existed.

She was Scythe's now. He was hers. She had to help him if she could.

Carefully, she retrieved the automatic rifle she had watched him stow on one of the wine racks. It wasn't her first time handling a large weapon. After Vito Massioni had nearly killed Pietro in Matera, she had taken it upon herself to learn a bit about self-defense, including how to shoot a firearm. Hitting the side of an unmoving barn was hardly preparation for the savagery she knew she would find outside the villa, but she had to try.

For Scythe—for the future she prayed they might

have together—she was willing to do and risk anything.

Holding on to their bond like a lifeline as well as a guide, she hurried out of the wine cellar and into the main area of the villa. All of the lights were out, everything cloaked in darkness. Everything except the flashes of gunfire exploding like fireworks on the back lawn of the house.

Oh, God.

Scythe.

She could feel that he was alive, but he was hurting. He was injured, but he was full of battle rage so sharp and violent, she felt it erupting within her too.

She wanted to unload her weapon into the fray.

She wanted to kill and punish and destroy.

Scythe's emotions, twining with her own.

She wasn't sure whose were the most ferocious.

On a guttural cry, she ran outside to the porch, the automatic rifle raised and poised to shoot. But she couldn't squeeze off a single shot. She stopped on the porch as surely as if she'd hit an invisible wall—blinded by the bright pops of light amid the inky darkness outside.

Each one seared her retinas, momentarily blinding her. She stood there, shaking with violence and nowhere for it to go. She was useless to Scythe when any errant bullet she fired could very likely hit him instead of the countless Rogues besieging him from all sides.

The rage inside her began to twist like a tempest. The strange hum she'd felt in the core of her being—in her marrow—now swelled into something bigger. Something too powerful for her to contain.

The hum became a whine, then a howl... then a scream.

It burst out of her in a gale force, a blast of energy and crippling sound she could not control.

Windows shattered all around her.

The headlights and windshield on the black sedan parked in the driveway exploded, sending pellets of glass skyrocketing into the night sky like glittering hail.

The gunfire ceased.

Everything seemed to slow down as her power overtook her.

Everything except for Scythe.

Only he seemed immune to power that flowed out of her. She saw him now, standing in the center of the battlefield, torn-up and bloodied, a crossbow hanging broken at his back, a long dagger gripped in his hand. His eyes were aglow, burning like lit coals in his skull. As the Rogues shrank back under Chiara's lengthening cry, several of their dark shapes skulking toward their escape, Scythe let out a bellow that shook the wooden planks beneath Chiara's feet.

And then he drew a semiautomatic pistol from somewhere on his body and opened fire on the retreating pack of Rogues, mowing down the entire lot of them with relentless, exacting aim.

Once she saw that he was okay—that he was alive—Chiara let go of her power and sagged back on her heels. Her breath raced in and out of her lungs. Her heart sped so fast it seemed to want to leap out of her chest.

She couldn't utter a word in that second. Whatever it was that had overtaken her sapped her of both her voice and her strength. Her head felt stuffed with cotton, her ears too. She had never felt so drained in her life.

No, not true.

She had felt this same odd miasma the night of the

attack, after she'd fended off her assailant with Sal's sword. Had she felt this swell of energy and sound on that night too? Maybe a little. She couldn't remember the details.

That awful night had been a blur. Her only concern had been the protection of her innocent son sleeping in the other room.

Tonight had been a glimpse of a different hell, seeing Scythe nearly overcome by so many Rogues. Fearing she could do nothing to help him. Horrified that he might die.

But he survived.

Thank God, they both had.

"Chiara!" His deep voice reached out to her through the darkness. She didn't realize it was out of fear until she felt the spike of his terror pierce the fog of her clouded senses. "Chiara—look out!"

A band of iron hooked her around the neck, yanking her off her feet.

She stumbled backward—into an immense wall of menace and seething madness.

Something cold jammed up tight against her temple.

"Stay right where you are," her attacker snarled at Scythe. "Drop your weapons on the ground—all of them. Take one goddamned step, you crippled fuck, and I'll paint this porch with the bitch's brains."

Scythe complied in utter silence. After shrugging the crossbow off his back, he placed two pistols and a couple of long daggers in the grass at his feet. Then he stood unmoving, his arms down at his sides. What her captor didn't seem to understand was that Scythe was no invalid in any sense of the word. He was a Gen One, and a former Hunter besides. Even with one hand, he was more lethal than ten Breed males like this scum who held her now.

But Scythe was worried for her. His fear for her could cost him.

"Scythe." She tried to tell him with her eyes, and with their bond, not to risk himself trying to save her.

If he felt her warning, he gave no sign.

Outside, he was the picture of careful surrender. Inside, beyond his concern, he was raging with animosity and the urge to deliver death in the worst way. His fury gave her hope, but it also terrified her. She knew he would only obey her assailant until the first inkling of opportunity presented itself. He would still give up his life if it meant saving hers.

When he finally spoke, his cool voice belied the tumult of his intentions. "Whatever you think this woman has done to wrong you, you're mistaken. She's innocent."

"Innocent." The male holding her practically spat the word. "Tell that to my brother. He'd be alive if not for her."

Chiara had to struggle to summon her voice. "I don't know what you're talking about. I don't know who you are. I never met your brother."

"Don't play dumb with me, bitch." The gun held to the side of her head dug deeper into her temple. "My brother, Luigi, was gunned down by the Order in that driveway out there six weeks ago. All because of you and that whelp of yours. Massioni should've killed both of you along with that piece of shit Sal Genova."

Luigi.

That was the name of one of the thugs Vito Massioni used to send out to the villa from time to time. She remembered Luigi now. He and the other Breed male who generally accompanied him on Massioni's orders used to enjoy intimidating her with innuendos and bullying threats about her little boy.

She had been glad to find out that Ettore had shot both of the men when he and Bella escaped Massioni and came to the vineyard to take Chiara and Pietro with them to a safe house.

Scythe's house, as it had turned out.

"If the Order killed your brother, take it up with them," Scythe said, his voice measured and cautious. "Put your blame where it belongs, not with a defenseless female."

"Defenseless?" Her captor chuckled. "There's plenty of fight in this one. I like it when they resist a little. Or a lot."

As if to demonstrate, her captor tightened his hold around her neck. She let out a choked gasp, wishing she had some reserves left of her power so she could blast him back to the hole he crawled out from under.

Scythe's blood answered her misery with a soothing calm that she felt as tangibly as if he'd touched her. She couldn't see his face through the darkness that shrouded him, but she felt his love. She felt his promise.

We'll come through this.

Together.

She nodded faintly, trust in him—in the promise of their love—buoying her.

"She's even lovelier up close, don't you agree?" The gun pressed to her temple now began to slide down the side of her face in an obscene caress. He skimmed it over her breast and down the front of her body. "I don't usually enjoy sloppy seconds, but I'll make an exception with her."

The nose of the gun drifted lower, toward her sex. Scythe growled, the first betrayal of his fury.

Her assailant's answering laughter was coarse with twisted glee. "Careful, now. You don't want to test me. I'll do whatever I want with her. She's all mine."

Chiara felt something flip inside Scythe. Her bond to him went electric. And then, just like that, he was airborne, leaping forward in one blinding motion. Her body listened to their bond, telling her instantly what to do. Perfectly in sync with him, as if it were a dance they had choreographed and practiced a thousand times, Chiara let her knees give way, dropping to the floor like a stone.

Scythe crashed into her captor, his right arm flat across the male's throat, driving him backward, into the wall. He had the gun stripped from his opponent's hand before Chiara realized it.

"You're wrong, you son of a bitch." Scythe jammed the pistol between the male's bulging eyes. He pulled the trigger and two shots slammed home. "She's mine."

CHAPTER 14

Scythe held Chiara against him under the warm spray of the shower. He didn't know how much time had passed since he'd carried her away from the carnage outside and into the house. He only knew that he never wanted to let her go again.

After tonight, nothing was ever going to separate them.

"It's over," he murmured, pressing a kiss to the top of her head. "I've got you now, angel."

And she had him... forever, if he had anything to say about it.

They were one. Her strong heartbeat confirmed his resolve, pounding in perfect cadence with his. Her blood was a bright force within him, so robust it took his breath away.

They had fortified their bond in the moments following tonight's attack. His wounds had been severe, but already he was healing, thanks to Chiara. His diminutive mate had saved him with her blood not once, but twice.

She had saved them both with the astonishing power of her Breedmate gift.

He was still marveling at the awesome energy she'd wielded at the height of the battle. The ferocity of it had been a revelation, not only to him, but to her. It was dimmed now, returned to the soothing vibration he'd felt humming along his senses ever since he'd taken his first taste of her blood.

She tipped her head up to look at him, her arms wrapped around him. "I was so scared, Scythe."

He brought his hand up to stroke her cheek. "You were miraculous. My miracle."

"I had no idea that power was inside me. The night Luigi's brother first broke into the villa, I remember screaming at him as I fended him off with Sal's sword. I remember feeling dazed and drained afterward, but I didn't know why. I thought it was an adrenaline crash. I thought I had been lucky that I was able to drive him away."

Scythe grunted, having more understanding now. "You *were* lucky. But you were also stronger than you knew."

"Your blood has made me stronger," she said, brushing her lips over his chest. "Your love has made me stronger, Scythe."

On a humbled groan, he cupped her beautiful face in his palm and drew her toward him for his kiss. As battered as he was from the fight, it was nothing compared to the devotion he felt for his woman. Nor was it any match for the desire he felt for her.

Bringing her close, he deepened the joining of their

mouths, need coiling within him. He felt hers inside him, too, and his body quickened with hunger.

He might have made love to her right then and there, if not for the sudden prickle of awareness that brought his head up with a start.

Chiara's eyes widened. "What is it?"

"Vehicles coming up the driveway outside."

A jolt of alarm shot through her veins and into him via their blood bond. "Not more Rogues?"

He shook his head, feeling no cause for concern. "No, not them. But we should get dressed. Come on."

By the time they emerged from the villa a moment later, Trygg and Savage were already out of the Order's black SUV and jogging up onto the porch. Garbed in combat gear and heavy weaponry, the two warriors gaped at Scythe and Chiara, who stood hand-in-hand waiting to greet them.

"Holy shit," Savage gasped.

Trygg ran a hand over his shaved head, then chuckled under his breath—one of the few times Scythe had ever seen his surly brother crack anything close to a smile.

The two warriors' gazes swept the moonlit lawn that was still smoking from the dozen Rogues that Scythe had ashed with titanium blades, arrows and bullets.

Savage blew out a low whistle. "You did all this by yourself?"

"I had some help," Scythe said, bringing his extraordinary Breedmate under the shelter of his arm.

Trygg and Savage exchanged a look.

"Commander Archer is going to be very interested to hear this story," Savage said. "Hell, so am I."

"Chiara and I will be glad to tell it, but first we need

to return to Rome. There's something more important we need to do there."

She glanced up at him, and he felt her joy—her relief—beaming up at him from her warm brown eyes. "We need to see Pietro. I need to see my son."

Scythe bent his head to hers, his mouth nestling beside her ear. "Our son, Chiara."

She drew back on an inhaled breath, elation radiating in her exquisite face. Then she threw her arms around his neck and kissed him like a woman possessed. Like a woman deeply, madly in love.

Scythe kissed her back with all the devotion his battered heart could hold.

His past had been hell. Tonight had been the closest he'd ever come to that place again. But now he knew what heaven was.

He was holding his own extraordinary piece of it in his arms.

And he was never letting her go.

EPILOGUE

Six months later…

"Push me higher!"

Scythe grinned and reached for the swing, gripping the wooden seat and pulling back before letting it fly. Pietro squealed with laughter, and he chuckled right along with him.

It was a beautiful evening in Potenza. Cool and breezy, the rolling vineyard hills and soft, cool grass of the lawn beneath his bare feet cast in the mystical blue of twilight. He inhaled the scent of turned, fertile earth and sweet Aglianico grapes.

The scent of home.

Pietro's giggles as Scythe sent him on another ride on the swing only fortified his contentment. And then there was Chiara.

"You two better think about coming in soon. The movie is about to start."

His mate's voice washed over him like soothing summer rain.

He turned and waved to her where she rocked in her own swing on the porch. A light shawl covered her shoulders, and her rich brown hair was piled in a loose bun on top of her head. His blood pulsed with desire. With love so deep it made him shake with the urge to cross the lawn and sweep her off to bed with him.

Would he ever tire of having her?

His pulse responded with a resounding, *"Never."*

"We'll be right in," he called back to her with a smile.

"One more push, Papa, please?" Pietro pleaded.

Scythe squeezed his eyes closed, his throat going tight. When they had returned to the vineyard from Rome and Pietro had learned that Scythe would be staying with them from then on, the little boy had gone very quiet. Chiara had explained that she and Scythe were mated, and that now they would be a family.

Pietro had been confused. "What do I call him?" he'd asked. Chiara handled it beautifully and with the utmost grace, as she did most things. She'd told her son that he should call him Scythe, and, then, perhaps someday, if he wanted to choose another name to call Scythe, he could do that when he was ready.

It had only been a week ago that Pietro had announced he didn't want to call him Scythe anymore, but he'd already had one father, and he was gone now. The boy thought what he could really use was a Papa. Would Scythe want to be his Papa?

Scythe had been moved more deeply than he thought possible. Hell, he still hadn't quite come to terms with it. After all the loss and suffering he'd known, this family was healing him more every day.

How strange that only a few short months ago, he'd viewed bonding and growing attached to others as a form of slavery... just another chain to hold him down, to weaken him. But the truth was, Chiara and her young son had set him free.

They had given his life meaning.

Soon, he would have one more reason to be grateful to his lovely, remarkable Chiara.

He couldn't keep his gaze from straying to her as she got up from the porch swing and stood. Her hand rested lovingly atop the bump of her belly where their child was growing. Her smile reached out to Scythe, bridging the distance. Calling him home to the heaven that awaited him inside the villa with her.

"Come on, Papa! One more time, please?"

Scythe scrubbed his hand through his short beard, then grabbed hold of Pietro's swing. "All right, son. But you'd better hang on tight. This time, you're going to touch the clouds."

~*~

The Hunters are coming!

Presenting an all-new Midnight Breed spinoff series
you won't want to miss…

The Hunter Legacy Series

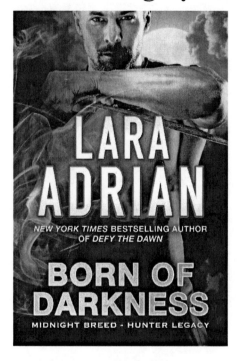

Born of Darkness
Coming Winter 2017

Thrilling standalone vampire romances from Lara Adrian
set in the Midnight Breed story universe.

For information on this series and more, visit:

www.LaraAdrian.com

Look for the next novel in the
Midnight Breed vampire romance series

Claimed in Shadows

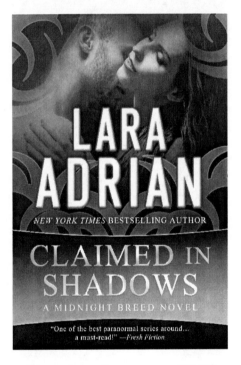

Coming Summer 2017

Releasing in ebook, trade paperback and audiobook.

For more information on the series and
upcoming releases, visit:

www.LaraAdrian.com

ABOUT THE AUTHOR

LARA ADRIAN is a New York Times and #1 international best-selling author, with nearly 4 million books in print and digital worldwide and translations licensed to more than 20 countries. Her books regularly appear in the top spots of all the major bestseller lists including the New York Times, USA Today, Publishers Weekly, Amazon.com, Barnes & Noble, etc. Reviewers have called Lara's books "addictively readable" (Chicago Tribune), "extraordinary" (Fresh Fiction), and "one of the consistently best" (Romance Novel News).

Writing as **TINA ST. JOHN,** her historical romances have won numerous awards including the National Readers Choice; Romantic Times Magazine Reviewer's Choice; Booksellers Best; and many others. She was twice named a Finalist in Romance Writers of America's RITA Awards, for Best Historical Romance (White Lion's Lady) and Best Paranormal Romance (Heart of the Hunter). More recently, the German translation of Heart of the Hunter debuted on Der Spiegel bestseller list.

Visit the author's website and sign up for new release announcements at www.LaraAdrian.com.

Find Lara on Facebook at
www.facebook.com/LaraAdrianBooks

Never miss a new book from Lara Adrian!

Sign up for the email newsletter at
www.LaraAdrian.com

Or type this URL into your web browser:
http://bit.ly/LaraAdrianNews

Be the first to get notified of Lara's new releases, plus be eligible for special subscribers-only exclusive content and giveaways that you won't find anywhere else.

Bonus!
When you confirm your subscription, you'll get an email with instructions for requesting free bookmarks and other fun goodies, while supplies last.

Sign up today!

To read more about Scythe and Chiara,
look for their introduction in

Midnight Untamed

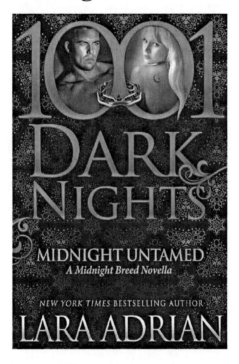

On sale now!

Available in ebook and trade paperback

For more information on the series and
upcoming releases, visit:

www.LaraAdrian.com

Thirsty for more Midnight Breed?

Read the complete series!

. . . and more to come!

Presenting a fun and relaxing new way to enjoy the Midnight Breed series!

The Midnight Breed Series Coloring Book

Featuring 21 coloring pages of original art and illustrations inspired by Lara Adrian's characters, book quotes and story world. With a variety of pages ranging from simple designs to intricate patterns, this book will keep you entertained for hours!

AVAILABLE NOW

If you enjoy sizzling contemporary romance,
don't miss this hot new series from Lara Adrian!

The 100 Series

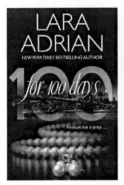 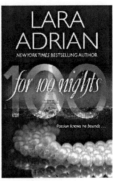

For 100 Days
For 100 Nights

Available in ebook, trade paperback and audiobook.

COMING SOON:

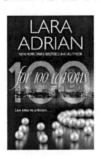

More romance and adventure from Lara Adrian!

Phoenix Code Series
(Paranormal Romantic Suspense)

"A fast-paced thrill ride." –Fresh Fiction

Masters of Seduction Series
(Paranormal Romance)

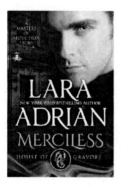 

"Thrilling, action-packed and super sexy." –Literal Addiction

Connect with Lara online at:

www.LaraAdrian.com

www.facebook.com/LaraAdrianBooks

www.goodreads.com/lara_adrian

www.twitter.com/lara_adrian

www.instagram.com/laraadrianbooks

www.pinterest.com/LaraAdrian

CPSIA information can be obtained
at www.ICGtesting.com
Printed in the USA
LVOW11s0332090817
544320LV00001B/184/P